THE PELICAN SHAKESPEARE

GENERAL EDITOR ALFRED HARBAGE

THE TRAGEDY OF

KING RICHARD THE SECOND

WILLIAM SHAKESPEARE

THE TRAGEDY OF KING RICHARD THE SECOND

EDITED BY MATTHEW W. BLACK

PENGUIN BOOKS

Penguin Books
625 Madison Avenue
New York, New York 10022

First published in *The Pelican Shakespeare* 1957
This revised edition first published 1970
Reprinted 1974, 1978, 1979

Library of Congress catalog card number: 78-98362

Printed in the United States of America by
Kingsport Press, Inc., Kingsport, Tennessee
Set in Monotype Ehrhardt

CONTENTS

Shakespeare and his Stage   7

The Texts of the Plays   12

Introduction   14

Note on the Text   22

The Tragedy of King Richard the Second   25

PUBLISHER'S NOTE

Soon after the thirty-eight volumes forming *The Pelican Shake-speare* had been published, they were brought together in *The Complete Pelican Shakespeare*. The editorial revisions and new textual features are explained in detail in the General Editor's Preface to the one-volume edition. They have all been incorporated in the present volume. The following should be mentioned in particular:

The lines are not numbered in arbitrary units. Instead all lines are numbered which contain a word, phrase, or allusion explained in the glossarial notes. In the occasional instances where there is a long stretch of unannotated text, certain lines are numbered in italics to serve the conventional reference purpose.

The intrusive and often inaccurate place-headings inserted by early editors are omitted (as is becoming standard practise), but for the convenience of those who miss them, an indication of locale now appears as first item in the annotation of each scene.

In the interest of both elegance and utility, each speech-prefix is set in a separate line when the speaker's lines are in verse, except when these words form the second half of a pentameter line. Thus the verse form of the speech is kept visually intact, and turned-over lines are avoided. What is printed as verse and what is printed as prose has, in general, the authority of the original texts. Departures from the original texts in this regard have only the authority of editorial tradition and the judgment of the Pelican editors; and, in a few instances, are admittedly arbitrary.

SHAKESPEARE AND
HIS STAGE

William Shakespeare was christened in Holy Trinity Church, Stratford-upon-Avon, April 26, 1564. His birth is traditionally assigned to April 23. He was the eldest of four boys and two girls who survived infancy in the family of John Shakespeare, glover and trader of Henley Street, and his wife Mary Arden, daughter of a small landowner of Wilmcote. In 1568 John was elected Bailiff (equivalent to Mayor) of Stratford, having already filled the minor municipal offices. The town maintained for the sons of the burgesses a free school, taught by a university graduate and offering preparation in Latin sufficient for university entrance; its early registers are lost, but there can be little doubt that Shakespeare received the formal part of his education in this school.

On November 27, 1582, a license was issued for the marriage of William Shakespeare (aged eighteen) and Ann Hathaway (aged twenty-six), and on May 26, 1583, their child Susanna was christened in Holy Trinity Church. The inference that the marriage was forced upon the youth is natural but not inevitable; betrothal was legally binding at the time, and was sometimes regarded as conferring conjugal rights. Two additional children of the marriage, the twins Hamnet and Judith, were christened on February 2, 1585. Meanwhile the prosperity of the elder Shakespeares had declined, and William was impelled to seek a career outside Stratford.

The tradition that he spent some time as a country

teacher is old but unverifiable. Because of the absence of records his early twenties are called the "lost years," and only one thing about them is certain – that at least some of these years were spent in winning a place in the acting profession. He may have begun as a provincial trouper, but by 1592 he was established in London and prominent enough to be attacked. In a pamphlet of that year, *Groats-worth of Wit*, the ailing Robert Greene complained of the neglect which university writers like himself had suffered from actors, one of whom was daring to set up as a playwright:

... an vpstart Crow, beautified with our feathers, that with his *Tygers hart wrapt in a Players hyde*, supposes he is as well able to bombast out a blanke verse as the best of you: and beeing an absolute *Iohannes fac totum*, is in his owne conceit the onely Shake-scene in a countrey.

The pun on his name, and the parody of his line "O tiger's heart wrapped in a woman's hide" (*3 Henry VI*), pointed clearly to Shakespeare. Some of his admirers protested, and Henry Chettle, the editor of Greene's pamphlet, saw fit to apologize:

... I am as sory as if the originall fault had beene my fault, because my selfe haue seene his demeanor no lesse ciuill than he excelent in the qualitie he professes: Besides, diuers of worship haue reported his vprightnes of dealing, which argues his honesty, and his facetious grace in writting, that approoues his Art. (Prefatory epistle, *Kind-Harts Dreame*)

The plague closed the London theatres for many months in 1592–94, denying the actors their livelihood. To this period belong Shakespeare's two narrative poems, *Venus and Adonis* and *The Rape of Lucrece*, both dedicated to the Earl of Southampton. No doubt the poet was rewarded with a gift of money as usual in such cases, but he did no further dedicating and we have no reliable information on whether Southampton, or anyone else, became his regular patron. His sonnets, first mentioned in 1598 and published without his consent in 1609, are intimate without being explicitly autobiographical. They seem to commemorate the poet's friendship with an idealized youth, rivalry with a more favored poet, and love affair with a dark mistress; and his bitterness when the mistress betrays him in conjunction with the friend; but it is difficult to decide precisely what the "story" is, impossible to decide whether it is fictional or true. The true distinction of the sonnets, at least of those not purely conventional, rests in the universality of the thoughts and moods they express, and in their poignancy and beauty.

In 1594 was formed the theatrical company known until 1603 as the Lord Chamberlain's men, thereafter as the King's men. Its original membership included, besides Shakespeare, the beloved clown Will Kempe and the famous actor Richard Burbage. The company acted in various London theatres and even toured the provinces, but it is chiefly associated in our minds with the Globe Theatre built on the south bank of the Thames in 1599. Shakespeare was an actor and joint owner of this company (and its Globe) through the remainder of his creative years. His plays, written at the average rate of two a year, together with Burbage's acting won it its place of leadership among the London companies.

Individual plays began to appear in print, in editions both honest and piratical, and the publishers became increasingly aware of the value of Shakespeare's name on the title pages. As early as 1598 he was hailed as the leading English dramatist in the *Palladis Tamia* of Francis Meres:

As *Plautus* and *Seneca* are accounted the best for Comedy and Tragedy among the Latines, so *Shakespeare* among the English is the most excellent in both kinds for the stage: for Comedy, witnes his *Gentlemen of Verona*, his *Errors*, his *Loue labors lost*, his *Loue labours wonne* [at one time in print but no longer extant, at least under this title], his *Midsummers night dream*, & his *Merchant of Venice*; for Tragedy, his *Richard the 2*, *Richard the 3*, *Henry the 4*, *King Iohn*, *Titus Andronicus*, and his *Romeo and Iuliet*.

9

The note is valuable both in indicating Shakespeare's pres-
tige and in helping us to establish a chronology. In the
second half of his writing career, history plays gave place
to the great tragedies; and farces and light comedies gave
place to the problem plays and symbolic romances. In
1623, seven years after his death, his former fellow-actors,
John Heminge and Henry Condell, cooperated with a
group of London printers in bringing out his plays in col-
lected form. The volume is generally known as the First
Folio.

Shakespeare had never severed his relations with Stratford. His wife and children may sometimes have shared
his London lodgings, but their home was Stratford. His
son Hamnet was buried there in 1596, and his daughters
Susanna and Judith were married there in 1607 and 1616
respectively. (His father, for whom he had secured a coat
of arms and thus the privilege of writing himself gentleman, died in 1601, his mother in 1608.) His considerable
earnings in London, as actor-sharer, part owner of the
Globe, and playwright, were invested chiefly in Stratford
property. In 1597 he purchased for £60 New Place, one of
the two most imposing residences in the town. A number
of other business transactions, as well as minor episodes in
his career, have left documentary records. By 1611 he was
in a position to retire, and he seems gradually to have
withdrawn from theatrical activity in order to live in
Stratford. In March, 1616, he made a will, leaving token
bequests to Burbage, Heminge, and Condell, but the bulk
of his estate to his family. The most famous feature of the
will, the bequest of the second-best bed to his wife, reveals
nothing about Shakespeare's marriage; the quaintness of
the provision seems commonplace to those familiar with
ancient testaments. Shakespeare died April 23, 1616, and
was buried in the Stratford church where he had been
christened. Within seven years a monument was erected
to his memory on the north wall of the chancel. Its por-
trait bust and the Droeshout engraving on the title page of

the First Folio provide the only likenesses with an established claim to authenticity. The best verbal vignette was written by his rival Ben Jonson, the more impressive for being imbedded in a context mainly critical:

... I loved the man, and doe honour his memory (on this side idolatry) as much as any. Hee was indeed honest, and of an open and free nature: had an excellent Phantsie, brave notions, and gentle expressions.... (*Timber or Discoveries*, ca. 1623–30)

*

The reader of Shakespeare's plays is aided by a general knowledge of the way in which they were staged. The King's men acquired a roofed and artificially lighted theatre only toward the close of Shakespeare's career, and then only for winter use. Nearly all his plays were designed for performance in such structures as the Globe – a three-tiered amphitheatre with a large rectangular platform extending to the center of its yard. The plays were staged by daylight, by large casts brilliantly costumed, but with only a minimum of properties, without scenery, and quite possibly without intermissions. There was a rear stage gallery for action "above," and a curtained rear recess for "discoveries" and other special effects, but by far the major portion of any play was enacted upon the projecting platform, with episode following episode in swift succession, and with shifts of time and place signaled the audience only by the momentary clearing of the stage between the episodes. Information about the identity of the characters and, when necessary, about the time and place of the action was incorporated in the dialogue. No place-headings have been inserted in the present editions; these are apt to obscure the original fluidity of structure, with the emphasis upon action and speech rather than scenic background. (Indications of place are supplied in the footnotes.) The acting, including that of the youthful apprentices to the profession who performed the parts of women, was highly skillful, with a premium placed upon grace of gesture and beauty of diction. The audiences, a cross section of the general public, commonly numbered a thousand, sometimes more than two thousand. Judged by the type of plays they applauded, these audiences were not only large but also perceptive.

THE TEXTS OF THE PLAYS

About half of Shakespeare's plays appeared in print for the first time in the folio volume of 1623. The others had been published individually, usually in quarto volumes, during his lifetime or in the six years following his death. The copy used by the printers of the quartos varied greatly in merit, sometimes representing Shakespeare's true text, sometimes only a debased version of that text. The copy used by the printers of the folio also varied in merit, but was chosen with care. Since it consisted of the best available manuscripts, or the more acceptable quartos (although frequently in editions other than the first), or of quartos corrected by reference to manuscripts, we have good or reasonably good texts of most of the thirty-seven plays.

In the present series, the plays have been newly edited from quarto or folio texts, depending, when a choice offered, upon which is now regarded by bibliographical specialists as the more authoritative. The ideal has been to reproduce the chosen texts with as few alterations as possible, beyond occasional relineation, expansion of abbreviations, and modernization of punctuation and spelling. Emendation is held to a minimum, and such material as has been added, in the way of stage directions and lines supplied by an alternative text, has been enclosed in square brackets.

None of the plays printed in Shakespeare's lifetime were divided into acts and scenes, and the inference is that the author's own manuscripts were not so divided. In the folio collection, some of the plays remained undivided, some were divided into acts, and some were divided into acts and scenes. During the eighteenth century all of the plays were divided into acts and scenes, and in the Cambridge edition of the mid-nineteenth century, from which the influential Globe text derived, this division was more or less regularized and the lines were numbered. Many useful works of reference employ the act–scene–line apparatus thus established.

Since this act–scene division is obviously convenient, but is of very dubious authority so far as Shakespeare's own structural principles are concerned, or the original manner of staging his plays, a problem is presented to modern editors. In the present series the act–scene division is retained marginally, and may be viewed as a reference aid like the line numbering. A star marks the points of division when these points have been determined by a cleared stage indicating a shift of time and place in the action of the play, or when no harm results from the editorial assumption that there is such a shift. However, at those points where the established division is clearly misleading – that is, where continuous action has been split up into separate "scenes" – the star is omitted and the distortion corrected. This mechanical expedient seemed the best means of combining utility and accuracy.

THE GENERAL EDITOR

INTRODUCTION

The increasing interest of thoughtful modern readers in *The Tragedy of King Richard the Second* is probably due in part to its unique position in Shakespeare's artistic development. Symbolic of this position is the fact that it is the only one of his better plays to be written entirely in verse. It would, perhaps, be fanciful to conclude that this is because poetry here plays a more functional role than in any of his other dramas. Yet the coincidence is striking, for *Richard II* is the first play in which Shakespeare makes his central figure an introspective, imaginative, and eloquent man – in short, a poet. This is the first of his characters into which he could freely have poured certain aspects of his own character and experience.

Richard is a lover of music, of pageantry, of luxurious hospitality; he is mercurial; he is highly self-conscious; he has the feeling for situations, the instinct for self-dramatization, of a born actor. It has indeed been supposed that Shakespeare the actor wrote the part for himself. We can at least agree that Richard is a person with whom Shakespeare as fact and tradition reveal him could eagerly have identified in these respects. If so, this may account for the unusual length of the part, and for the impression recorded by critics as diverse in temper as Coleridge and Sir Edmund Chambers that Richard is drawn with a skill unequalled except perhaps in *King Lear*, "a work of art and of love." It is worth remembering also that when some five years later Shakespeare next turned to a story in which the central figure was a self-conscious, sensitive, imaginative, and eloquent young prince, the result was the longest of all Shakespearean roles and the most popular, Hamlet.

At all events, the king's poetic nature is all-important in the total effect of *Richard II*. The story is that of a youthful, thoughtless, extravagant, and willfully unjust king who is responsible for the murder of his good uncle, Thomas, Duke of Gloucester, and the confiscation of his cousin Bolingbroke's estates, but whose dethronement leads eventually to the long and bloody Wars of the Roses,* and who in his fall becomes a sympathetic figure – in the eyes of his French biographers, indeed, a martyr. This seemingly impossible transformation is effected by exhibiting in the first two acts Richard's weakness as a king, and progressively thereafter his charm as a man. And the essence of that charm is that he is a poet, a minor poet, to be sure, a self-conscious, artificial poet, overfond of words and of rhetorical devices, but enough of a poet to win our hearts and make us forget how richly he deserves to be deposed.

But Richard's is one of the kinds of poetry with which his creator was experimenting toward the end of 1595, when *Richard II* was written, and therein lies the significance of the play in Shakespeare's progress as an artist. No thoughtful reader of Shakespeare's early work can resist the impression that his natural bent was toward poetry, and that he learned the dramatist's trade, the constructing of a theatrically effective plot, slowly and with conscious effort. Pegasus was never allowed to run away with the team, for that would have courted failure in the theatre, but his irresponsibility is evident in the unconvincing lyricism of Tyrrel's report of the murderers in *Richard III*, IV, iii, or of Mercutio's speech about Queen Mab in

---

* The subject of Shakespeare's earlier tetralogy, *1*, *2*, and *3 Henry VI* and *Richard III*.

Romeo and Juliet, I, iv, some forty lines of delightful fantasy which merely retard the plot. In the other plays of the so-called "lyrical group" written between 1593 and 1596, Shakespeare finds other important and legitimate uses for poetry in drama. But only Richard II, both protagonist and poet, allows his creator's winged horse full rein.

Thus with the economy of genius Shakespeare here solves two problems, one professional and the other personal, with a single stroke. Some of the satisfaction he must have felt is apparent in the profusion and splendor of the imagery in the play, in the intricate interweaving of image-patterns, and in the symmetry with which the images point up every stage in what Holinshed called God's "advancing" of Bolingbroke and "dejecting" of Richard. A good example is the emblematic transference of the sun from Richard (II, iv, 21 ; III, ii, 36 ff. ; III, iii, 62 ff., 178 ff.) to Bolingbroke (IV, i, 260–62). Many other skeins of imagery may be traced through the play, such as the rise and fall of Fortune's buckets, the "theatre-like state," and the neglected or well-tended garden. But nothing is more delusory than the supposition that the poet deliberately planned these patterns; they illustrate the instinctive workings of his poetic imagination.

As implied above, *Richard II* is artistically akin to a cluster of plays which can be assigned with some confidence to the years 1593–96. It has much in common also (though less than the other plays of the "lyrical group" because of its paucity of love scenes) with his sonnets, many of which presumably belong to the same period, since we hear of them circulating "among his private friends" as early as 1598. These relationships, together with an admittedly equivocal reference to the private presentation of a "King Richard" in 1595, impel the majority of recent editors to assign the composition of the piece to the latter year. It came at a time when the aged Elizabeth I and her councillors were extremely sensitive to the possible political repercussions of stage plays. Consequently when it appeared in print in 1597 the actual dethronement (IV, i, 154–318) had been excised. It had almost certainly been included in the stage performances and may well have been banned by the censor of books for that very reason. It was not printed until 1608, when Elizabeth's successor, James I, was firmly seated on the English throne.

As for the queen's anxiety, the perspective of three and a half centuries makes clear that while, like every re-enactment of history, the play had political meaning, it can have had no political purpose, and that, in supposing it could be useful as propaganda, both her majesty's government and the opposition were deceived. It is a vivid, impartial re-creation of a political impasse which brought death to a tyrant, but to a usurper a troublesome reign, and to the realm eventually some thirty years of civil war. It *is* full of conflicting political ideas : the divine right of kings, the subject's duty of passive obedience, the dangers of irresponsible despotism, the complex qualities of an ideal ruler. But which of these ideas were Shakespeare's own is impossible to discern. On politics as on religion he preserves as always "the taciturnity of nature." What can be said of this aspect of *Richard II* is that here, as in all the histories, Shakespeare wrote as a true patriot and that England was the heroine. The continuing power of the play to interest audiences in England and elsewhere can come only from its universal human appeal as drama.

That *Richard II* was also planned as the first part of a great tetralogy completed in *1* and *2 Henry IV* and *Henry V*, is far from certain, although this view has been brilliantly maintained by recent scholars. Carlisle's prophecy (IV, i, 114–49, 322–23) does indeed foretell the woes to come in Henry VI and Richard III's time, while Richard himself (V, i, 57–65) predicts to one of the actual rebels the treacherous rebellion of the Percies in *1 Henry IV* :

The time shall not be many hours of age
More than it is, ere foul sin gathering head
Shall break into corruption. Thou shalt think,
Though he divide the realm and give thee half,
It is too little, helping him to all.
And he shall think that thou, which knowest the way
To plant unrightful kings, wilt know again,
Being ne'er so little urged another way,
To pluck him headlong from the usurped throne.

Henry at the beginning of V, iii does foreshadow the character of Prince Hal in the next two histories as well as his transformation into the hero of *Henry V*. Many passages in the later three "parts" link them *retrospectively* with *Richard II*. But in the Hotspur of *Richard II* there is hardly any trace of the "gunpowder Percy" of *1 Henry IV*, and there is no hint anywhere of Falstaff. Highly qualified critics of the consecutive performance of the four pieces at Stratford in 1951 have commented that when played as a prologue to the tetralogy, *Richard II* becomes rather the rise of Bolingbroke than the tragedy of Richard, and such a reading is difficult to reconcile with the impression of Richard dwelt upon above. Perhaps the safest guess is that before writing *Richard II* the dramatist had in mind the whole framework of events as it was presented to him in his chronicle sources, but not the details of his characters and scenes. The four plays, though intricately and strongly connected, fall short of complete artistic unity.

The principal source of *Richard II* is the second edition (1587) of a popular compilation called *The Chronicles of England* by Raphael Holinshed, which provides the outlines of the events and characters. But there is evidence in both the plot and the dialogue that Shakespeare knew, and remembered striking details from, practically all the different versions of Richard's story available to him: the chronicles of Froissart and of Edward Hall; two or three French accounts of the deposition, favorable to Richard;

the *Mirror for Magistrates*; the first four books of Samuel
Daniel's poetical history of *The Civil Wars*; an earlier play,
Woodstock, which deals with the murder of the Duke of
Gloucester; and just possibly another earlier play on
Richard II, of which however no record remains. It would
be an obvious exaggeration to say that Shakespeare "did
the research" on his subject with the thoroughness of a
historian. He may, for example, have known *Woodstock*
simply through having acted in it. But it is no less misleading to suppose that he was content with Holinshed's
rather pedestrian narrative.

As usual, too, he altered history for dramatic effect,
though in this instance without damage to the enduring
truth of his picture. He also added brilliant improvisations
not found in any of his sources: the conversation between
Gaunt and the widowed Duchess of Gloucester (I, ii);
Gaunt's deathbed speech and the conference of Northumberland, Ross, and Willoughby (II, i); the several ap-
pearances of the queen, especially in the Duke of York's
garden at Langley (III, iv); the conception of Isabella as
having the maturity and vitality of Richard's first queen,
Anne of Bohemia, whereas she was in fact a child of eight
when he married her; the deposition scene; the appearance
of the Duchess of York to plead for her "son," Aumerle
(he was actually her stepson); the presentation of Richard's
coffin to Henry in the final scene. Unless the "old play"
on Richard II should somewhere miraculously turn up,
and prove to contain hints for all these alterations and
additions, we must describe at least a quarter of the play as
Shakespeare's invention.

The early stage history of *Richard II* is of unusual interest. Elizabeth herself exclaimed against it: "I am
Richard II, know ye not that? . . . This tragedy was played
forty times in open streets and houses." Even if we dis-
count "forty" as a common round number, an angry exaggeration, or both, Dover Wilson's statement that the

play "took London by storm" seems amply justified. Two new editions came out in a single year, 1598. In a poetical miscellany of 1600, more excerpts were included from *Richard II* than from any other drama. On Saturday, February 7, 1601, a performance by Shakespeare's company at the Globe was paid for by supporters of the Earl of Essex to stir up popular feeling in favor of his ill-starred attempt to seize the throne, and although the gentlemen who bespoke the performance were tried and punished, Shakespeare and his company apparently were not. On September 30, 1607, the piece was played by the crew of a ship en route to the West Indies. New editions were printed in 1608, 1615, 1623 (in the first folio), and 1634. In the summer of 1631 the Master of the Revels had £5 6s. 6d. from a benefit production at the Globe.

During the Restoration, the eighteenth, and the early nineteenth century at least six different stage adaptations of it were put on with some success in England and America. The chief Shakespearean actors of their respective centuries, Garrick (whose friend Dr Johnson disliked the play) and Irving (who planned a production but never put it on), are absent from the list of stars who have essayed the title role since 1700. But it has attracted such famous names as Macready, Edmund Kean, Wallack, Charles Kean, Junius Brutus Booth the elder, Edwin Booth, Benson, Granville-Barker, Beerbohm Tree, John Gielgud, Maurice Evans, Alec Guinness, and Michael Redgrave. In the twentieth-century American revival of 1937–38, directed by Miss Margaret Webster, Evans played it over three hundred times, and seemingly won for it some measure of continuing popularity on the stage and in television.

Curiously enough, considering its earlier and later success, until the third decade of the present century *Richard II* ranked well below several of Shakespeare's other histories – notably *1 Henry IV*, *Henry V*, and *Richard III* – in popularity on the stage. Critics have found it wanting in dramatic action, arresting characters (except Richard himself), and comic relief. But producers have been able to counterbalance these defects by spectacular staging of the pageantry of the tournament (I, iii) and – in an interpolated "episode" – of Richard's entry into London (V, ii); by expert playing of such scenes as the tearful interview of Gaunt and the Duchess of Gloucester (I, ii), the garden scene (III, iv), and Richard's farewell to his queen (V, i), which certainly lend variety of effect; and sometimes – though with questionable propriety – by portraying York throughout, and his duchess in V, ii, iii, as mildly humorous.

But on the stage, and even more surely for the reader, the play has its great moments. It is, in the words of Henry Morley, "full of passages that have floated out of their place in the drama to live in the minds of the people." Chief among these is John of Gaunt's apostrophe to England (II, i, 40 ff.), which even in American performances usually evokes a solid round of applause. And there are others: Saintsbury calls York's description of "our two cousins coming into London" (especially V, ii, 23–36) the most famous passage in the play; the pathos of Richard's soliloquy in prison (V, v, 1–66) has been highly praised, as have his monody on the divine right of kings (III, ii, 36–62) and that on the irony of kingship (III, ii, 144–70), the Bishop of Carlisle's prophecy (IV, i, 114–49), and Bolingbroke's forthright, vividly human rejection of the consolations of philosophy (I, iii, 294–303).

It would be a feeble actor who could not hold his audience, and an unimaginative reader who felt no thrill in the great moments of Richard's story: his passionate outbursts of hope and despair when he returns from Ireland, as Salisbury and then Scroop reluctantly tell of the disbanding of his Welsh army, the flocking of his subjects to Bolingbroke, and the deaths of his favorites; his cry as he descends to parley with the usurper, "Down, down I come, like glist'ring Phaethon"; above all, his tragic eloquence as he dramatizes his abdication before the Parliament which had so recently been his, and under the inscrutable eye of the "silent king."

University of Pennsylvania   MATTHEW W. BLACK

NOTE ON THE TEXT

The present edition follows the text of the first quarto, 1597, which appears to have been printed from the author's draft. The abdication speeches, IV, i, 154–318, have been added from the text in the folio, 1623, which, though printed in the main from one of the later quartos of the play, was evidently corrected – especially in these speeches – by means of a playhouse prompt-copy. The speeches had first been printed in the fourth quarto, 1608, but with mislinings and omissions indicative of faulty copy. Nonetheless, many modern editions, including the present one, prefer some thirteen fourth-quarto readings. The quartos are not divided into acts and scenes. The act–scene division here supplied marginally follows the division in the folio except that V, iii is split into V, iii and iv, thus giving six scenes for this act instead of the five in the folio.

Below is a list of the substantive departures from the copy-texts, i.e. the folio of 1623 (F) for IV, i, 154–318, and the quarto of 1597 as press-corrected in all extant copies (Q). The adopted reading in italics with an indication of its source – usually the quartos of 1598 (Q2) and (Q3), of 1608 (Q4), of 1615 (Q5), and of 1634 (Q6), or the folios and early editors – is followed by the reading of the copy-texts in roman. Expansions of unmistakable abbreviations and corrections of obvious printing errors are not listed.

I, i, 118 *by my* (F) by (Q)   162 *Harry, when?* (Pope) Harry ? when (Q)   178 *reputation. That* (F) Reputation that (Q)
I, ii, 47 *sit* (F) set (Q)   58 *it* (Q2) is (Q)   60 *begun* (Q2) begone (Q)

I, iii, 15 *thee* (Q2) the (Q)   33 *comest* (Q5) comes (Q)   43 *daring-hardy* (Theobald) daring, hardy, (Q)   58 *thee* (Q3) the (Q)   172 *then but* (F) but (Q)   180 *you owe* (F) y'owe (Q)   193 *far* (F2) fare (Q)   222 *night* (Q4) nightes (Q)   239 *had it* (Theobald) had't (Q)   289 *strewed* (Malone) strowd (Q)   308 *Where'er* (Q2) Where eare (Q)

I, iv, 20 *cousin,* (F) Coosens (Q)   52 s.d. *Enter Bushy* (F) Enter Bushy with newes (Q)   53 *Bushy, what news* (F) omitted (Q)

II, i, 15 *life's* (Rowe) liues (Q)   18 *fond* (Collier conj.; Camb.) found (Q)   19 *metres* (Steevens conj.; Malone) meeters (Q)   48 *a moat* (Q4) moat (Q)   85 *No, misery* (Q3) No misery (Q)   102 *incagèd* (Dyce) inraged (Q)   113 *now, not* (Theobald) now not, not (Q)   124 *brother* (Q2) brothers (Q)   130 *precedent* (Pope) president (Q)   168 *my own* (all but Petworth copy of Q) his own (Petworth copy)   177 *the* (F) a (Q)   229 *Ere't* (F) Eart (Q)   257 *king's* (Q3) King (Q)   277 *Blanc* (Camb. ii) Blan (Q)   280 *The son and heir of the Earl of Arundel* (supplied by Halliwell; not in early texts)   284 *Coint* (Halliwell) Coines (Q)   294 *gilt* (F) guilt (Q)

II, ii, 16 *eye* (F) eyes (Q)   25 *More's* (F) more is (Q)   31 *though in* (Collier) though on (Q2) thought on (Q)   39 *known – what* (Capell) knowen what (Q)   53 *Henry* (Var. 1821) H. (Q)   112 *Th' one* (F) T one (Q)   129 *that's* (F) that is (Q)   148 *Bagot* (White) omitted (Q)

II, iii, 9 *Cotswold* (Hanmer) Cotshall (Q)   25 *Why,* (Q3) Why (Q)   30 *lordship* (Q2) Lo: (Q)   36 *Hereford, boy?* (Q3) Herefords boy. (Q)

II, iv, 8 *all are* (Q2) are al (Q)

III, ii, 31 *offer* (Pope) offer, (Q)   32 *succor* (Pope) succors (Q)   40 *boldly* (Collier conj.; Hudson) bouldy (Q)   72 *O'erthrows* (F) Ouerthrowes (Q)   130 *won* (Q3) woon (Q)   134 *this offense* (F) this (Q)   170 *through* (Q2) thorough (Q)

III, iii, 13 *brief with you to* (F) brief to (Q)   59 *rain* (F) raigne (Q)   119 *a prince and just* (Sisson) princesse iust (Q)   202 *hand* (F) handes (Q)

III, iv, 11 *joy?* (Var. 1773) griefe (Q)   26 *pins* (F) pines (Q)   28 *change:* (F) change (Q)   29 *yon* (Q2) yong (Q)   55 *seized* (Q3) ceasde (Q)   57 *garden! We at* (Capell) garden at (Q)   80 *Cam'st* (Q2) Canst (Q)   85 *lord's* (F) Lo: (Q)

IV, i, 22 *him* (Q3) them (Q)   43 *Fitzwater* (F) Fitzwaters (Q)   54 *As* (Johnson) As it (Q)   55 *sun . . . sun* (Capell) sinne . . . sinne

23

(Q) *is my* (Q3) is (Q)   109 *thee* (Q2) the (Q)   114 *Marry* (F3) Mary (Q)   145 *you* (Q2) yon (Q)   165 *limbs* (Q4) knee (F)   183 *and on* (Q4) on (F)   *yours* (Q4) thine (F)   199 *tend* (Q4) 'tend (F) 210 *duty's* (Var. 1821) duties (Q4) dutious (F)   *rites* (Q4) Oathes (F)   215 *that swear* (Q4) are made (F)   229 *folly* (Q4) follyes (F)   237 *upon* (Q4) upon me (F)   250 *To undeck* (Q4) T'vndeck (F)   251 *and* (Q4) a (F)   255 *Nor* (Q4) No, nor (F) 260 *mockery king* (Q4) Mockerie, King (F)   267 *bankrout* (Q4) Bankrupt (F)   276 *the* (Q4) that (F)   285 *Was* (Q4) Is (F)   *that* (Q4) which (F)   286 *And* (Q4) That (F)   289 *a* (Q4) an (F)   296 *manners* (Q4) manner (F)   319 *On Wednesday next* (Q4) Let it be so, and loe on Wednesday next (Q)   333 *I will lay* (Pope) Ile lay (Q)

V, i, 32 *correction mildly* (Neilson) correction, mildly (Q)   41 *thee* (Q2) the (Q)   62 *And he* (Keightly conj. ; Wilson) He (Q)

V, ii, 2 *off* (F) of (Q)   11 *thee* (F) the (Q)   17 *thee ! Welcome* (Theobald) the Welcome (Q)   65 *bond* (F) band (Q)   94 *thee* (Q2) the (Q)   116 *And* (Q2) An (Q)

V, iii, 36 *that I may* (Q2) that May (Q)   43 *foolhardy* (Rolfe) foole, hardie (Q)   51 *passed* (Dyce) past (Q)   68 *And* (Q2) An (Q)   75 *voiced* (Q3) voice (Q)   111 *King Henry* (Q2) Yorke (Q)   135–36 *With all my heart I pardon him* (Pope) I pardon him with all my heart (Q)

V, v, 20 *through* (F) thorow (Q)   27 *sit* (Q3) set (Q)   79 *bestrid* (F) bestride (Q)

V, vi, 12 s.d. *Fitzwater* (Q6) Fitzwaters (Q)   25 *reverend* (Q3) reuerent (Q)   43 *thorough* (Camb.) through (Q)

THE TRAGEDY OF
KING RICHARD
THE SECOND

King Richard II
John of Gaunt, Duke of Lancaster ⎫
Edmund of Langley, Duke of York ⎬ uncles to the King
Henry, surnamed Bolingbroke, Duke of Hereford, son to
   John of Gaunt ; afterwards King Henry IV
Duke of Aumerle, son to the Duke of York
Thomas Mowbray, Duke of Norfolk
Duke of Surrey
Earl of Salisbury
Lord Berkeley
Bushy ⎫
Bagot ⎬ servants to King Richard
Green ⎭
Earl of Northumberland
Henry Percy, surnamed Hotspur, his son
Lord Ross
Lord Willoughby
Lord Fitzwater
Bishop of Carlisle
Abbot of Westminster
Lord Marshal
Sir Stephen Scroop
Sir Pierce of Exton
Captain of a band of Welshmen
Gardener and his Men
Queen to King Richard
Duchess of York
Duchess of Gloucester
Ladies attending on the Queen
Lords, Heralds, Officers, Soldiers, Keeper, Messenger,
   Groom, and other Attendants

Scene : *England and Wales*]

THE TRAGEDY OF
KING RICHARD
THE SECOND

I, i

*Enter King Richard, John of Gaunt, with other
Nobles and Attendants.*

KING

Old John of Gaunt, time-honored Lancaster,   1
Hast thou, according to thy oath and band,   2
Brought hither Henry Hereford, thy bold son,
Here to make good the boist'rous late appeal,   4
Which then our leisure would not let us hear,   5
Against the Duke of Norfolk, Thomas Mowbray?

GAUNT

I have, my liege.

KING

Tell me, moreover, hast thou sounded him
If he appeal the duke on ancient malice,   9
Or worthily, as a good subject should,   10
On some known ground of treachery in him?

GAUNT

As near as I could sift him on that argument,
On some apparent danger seen in him   13

I, i A room of state (Holinshed's *Chronicles*, Shakespeare's principal source
for *Richard II*, locates this scene 'within the castle of Windsor,' where the
king and his nobles sat on 'a great scaffold,' and gives the time as the latter
part of April, 1398) **s.d.** *Gaunt* Ghent (his birthplace) 1 *time-honored*
venerable (he was actually fifty-eight) 2 *band* bond (Gaunt was a pledge
for Bolingbroke's appearance) 4 *appeal* accusation (here of treason) made
by one who undertook under penalty to prove it 5 *our . . . us* (the royal
plural); *leisure* i.e. lack of leisure 9 *appeal* accuse; *malice* enmity 10
worthily justly 13 *apparent* obvious

Aimed at your highness, no inveterate malice.

KING

Then call them to our presence.   *[Exit Attendant.]*
                              Face to face,
And frowning brow to brow, ourselves will hear
The accuser and the accusèd freely speak.

18   High-stomached are they both and full of ire,
In rage deaf as the sea, hasty as fire.

Enter Bolingbroke and Mowbray.

BOLINGBROKE

Many years of happy days befall
My gracious sovereign, my most loving liege!

MOWBRAY

Each day still better other's happiness

23   Until the heavens, envying earth's good hap,
24   Add an immortal title to your crown!

KING

We thank you both. Yet one but flatters us,

26   As well appeareth by the cause you come –
Namely, to appeal each other of high treason.

28   Cousin of Hereford, what dost thou object
Against the Duke of Norfolk, Thomas Mowbray?

BOLINGBROKE

First – heaven be the record to my speech! –
In the devotion of a subject's love,

32   Tend'ring the precious safety of my prince
33   And free from other, misbegotten hate,
34   Come I appellant to this princely presence.
Now, Thomas Mowbray, do I turn to thee,
And mark my greeting well; for what I speak
My body shall make good upon this earth
Or my divine soul answer it in heaven.

---

18 *High-stomached* haughty   **23** *hap* luck   **24** *immortal title* i.e. angel or
saint   **26** *cause you come* matter you come about   **28** *what . . . object* what
accusation do you make   **32** *Tend'ring* being lovingly mindful of   **33**
misbegotten of any other kind than that begotten of love for the king   **34**
appellant as accuser

Thou art a traitor and a miscreant,   39
Too good to be so, and too bad to live,
Since the more fair and crystal is the sky,
The uglier seem the clouds that in it fly.
Once more, the more to aggravate the note,   43
With a foul traitor's name stuff I thy throat
And wish, so please my sovereign, ere I move,
What my tongue speaks my right-drawn sword may   46
     prove.

MOWBRAY
Let not my cold words here accuse my zeal.   47
'Tis not the trial of a woman's war,   48
The bitter clamor of two eager tongues,   49
Can arbitrate this cause betwixt us twain;
The blood is hot that must be cooled for this.
Yet can I not of such tame patience boast
As to be hushed and naught at all to say.
First, the fair reverence of your highness curbs me
From giving reins and spurs to my free speech,
Which else would post until it had returned   56
These terms of treason doubled down his throat.
Setting aside his high blood's royalty,
And let him be no kinsman to my liege,
I do defy him and I spit at him,
Call him a slanderous coward and a villain;
Which to maintain, I would allow him odds
And meet him, were I tied to run afoot   63
Even to the frozen ridges of the Alps,
Or any other ground inhabitable   65
Where ever Englishman durst set his foot.
Meantime let this defend my loyalty:
By all my hopes, most falsely doth he lie.

---

39 *miscreant* un-Christian villain   43 *note* charge (of treason)   46 *right-drawn* drawn in a just cause   47 *accuse my zeal* cast doubt upon my ardor or loyalty   48 *woman's war* war of words   49 *eager* sharp   56 *post* ride at high speed   63 *tied* under bond   65 *inhabitable* uninhabitable

BOLINGBROKE

69   Pale trembling coward, there I throw my gage,
70   Disclaiming here the kinred of the king,
     And lay aside my high blood's royalty,
72   Which fear, not reverence, makes thee to except.
     If guilty dread have left thee so much strength
74   As to take up mine honor's pawn, then stoop.
     By that and all the rites of knighthood else,
     Will I make good against thee, arm to arm,
77   What I have spoke or thou canst worse devise.

MOWBRAY

     I take it up; and by that sword I swear
     Which gently laid my knighthood on my shoulder,
     I'll answer thee in any fair degree
     Or chivalrous design of knightly trial;
82   And when I mount, alive may I not light
     If I be traitor or unjustly fight!

KING

     What doth our cousin lay to Mowbray's charge?
85   It must be great that can inherit us
     So much as of a thought of ill in him.

BOLINGBROKE

87   Look what I speak, my life shall prove it true –
88   That Mowbray hath received eight thousand nobles
89   In name of lendings for your highness' soldiers,
90   The which he hath detained for lewd employments,
     Like a false traitor and injurious villain.
     Besides I say, and will in battle prove –
93   Or here, or elsewhere to the furthest verge
     That ever was surveyed by English eye –
95   That all the treasons for these eighteen years

---

69 *gage* glove in token of defiance   70 *kinred* kinship   72 *except* use as an exception   74 *mine honor's pawn* i.e. the gage   77 *or . . . devise* or anything worse you can imagine I have said   82 *light* dismount   85–86 *inherit us . . . of* make us have   87 *Look what* whatever   88 *nobles* gold coins worth 6s. 8d. each   89 *lendings* pay advanced when regular pay cannot be given   90 *lewd* base   93 *Or* either   95 *eighteen years* (since the commons' revolt of 1381)

Complotted and contrivèd in this land
Fetch from false Mowbray their first head and spring.   97
Further I say, and further will maintain,   98
Upon his bad life to make all this good,
That he did plot the Duke of Gloucester's death,   100
Suggest his soon-believing adversaries,   101
And consequently, like a traitor coward,   102
Sluiced out his innocent soul through streams of blood;
Which blood, like sacrificing Abel's, cries,
Even from the tongueless caverns of the earth,
To me for justice and rough chastisement;   106
And, by the glorious worth of my descent,
This arm shall do it, or this life be spent.

KING

How high a pitch his resolution soars!   109
Thomas of Norfolk, what say'st thou to this?

MOWBRAY

O, let my sovereign turn away his face
And bid his ears a little while be deaf,
Till I have told this slander of his blood   113
How God and good men hate so foul a liar!

KING

Mowbray, impartial are our eyes and ears.
Were he my brother, nay, my kingdom's heir,
As he is but my father's brother's son,
Now by my sceptre's awe I make a vow,   118
Such neighbor nearness to our sacred blood
Should nothing privilege him nor partialize   120
The unstooping firmness of my upright soul.

---

97 *head* source   98–99 *maintain . . . good* undertake to prove, by ending his wicked life   100 *Duke of Gloucester's death* (at Calais, while Mowbray was in command there; Gloucester was Richard's uncle and severest critic, and it is probable that the king ordered his execution)   101 *Suggest . . . adversaries* put his easily persuaded enemies up to it   102 *consequently* subsequently and as a result   106 *To me* (spoken with menacing emphasis, aimed at Richard)   109 *pitch* peak of a falcon's flight   1.3 *danger of* disgrace to   118 *my . . . awe* the reverence due my sceptre   120 *partialize* make partial, bias

He is our subject, Mowbray; so art thou :
Free speech and fearless I to thee allow.

MOWBRAY

Then, Bolingbroke, as low as to thy heart
Through the false passage of thy throat, thou liest !
126 Three parts of that receipt I had for Calais
Disbursed I duly to his highness' soldiers.
The other part reserved I by consent,
129 For that my sovereign liege was in my debt
130 Upon remainder of a dear account
131 Since last I went to France to fetch his queen.
Now swallow down that lie ! For Gloucester's death,
133 I slew him not, but, to my own disgrace,
Neglected my sworn duty in that case.
For you, my noble Lord of Lancaster,
The honorable father to my foe,
Once did I lay an ambush for your life –
A trespass that doth vex my grievèd soul ;
But ere I last received the sacrament,
140 I did confess it and exactly begged
Your grace's pardon, and I hope I had it.
142 This is my fault. As for the rest appealed,
It issues from the rancor of a villain,
144 A recreant and most degenerate traitor ;
145 Which in myself I boldly will defend,
146 And interchangeably hurl down my gage
Upon this overweening traitor's foot
To prove myself a loyal gentleman
Even in the best blood chambered in his bosom.

126 *that receipt I had* the money I received   129 *For that* because   130 *dear account* heavy debt   131 *Since . . . queen* since my latest voyage in furtherance of Richard's marriage to Isabella of France   133–34 *I . . . case* (Mowbray speaks ambiguously; there is some evidence that he postponed the execution, and he probably did not actually perform it)   140 *exactly* completely and expressly   142 *rest appealed* remainder of the charge   144 *recreant* cowardly   145 *Which* which assertion   146 *interchangeably* in turn

In haste whereof most heartily I pray   150
Your highness to assign our trial day.

KING

Wrath-kindled gentlemen, be ruled by me ;
Let's purge this choler without letting blood.   153
This we prescribe, though no physician ;
Deep malice makes too deep incision.
Forget, forgive ; conclude and be agreed ;   156
Our doctors say this is no month to bleed.   157
Good uncle, let this end where it begun ;
We'll calm the Duke of Norfolk, you your son.

GAUNT

To be a make-peace shall become my age.   160
Throw down, my son, the Duke of Norfolk's gage.

KING

And, Norfolk, throw down his.

GAUNT   When, Harry, when ?
Obedience bids I should not bid again.

KING

Norfolk, throw down, we bid. There is no boot.   164

MOWBRAY

Myself I throw, dread sovereign, at thy foot.
My life thou shalt command, but not my shame.
The one my duty owes ; but my fair name,
Despite of death that lives upon my grave,   168
To dark dishonor's use thou shalt not have.
I am disgraced, impeached, and baffled here ;   170
Pierced to the soul with slander's venomed spear,
The which no balm can cure but his heart-blood   172
Which breathed this poison.   173

---

150 *In haste whereof* to speed which proof   153 *choler* anger; *letting blood*
bleeding medicinally, with a quibble on bloodshed in combat   156
conclude make terms   157 *no month to bleed* (the almanacs prescribed
certain seasons as favorable for bleeding)   160 *shall* will certainly   164
boot help for it   168 *Despite . . . lives* that will live, in spite of death   170
impeached accused; *baffled* publicly disgraced   172–73 *his heart-blood*
Which the heart-blood of that man who   173 *breathed* uttered

KING   Rage must be withstood.
174   Give me his gage. Lions make leopards tame.

MOWBRAY
Yea, but not change his spots! Take but my shame,
And I resign my gage. My dear dear lord,
The purest treasure mortal times afford
Is spotless reputation. That away,
Men are but gilded loam or painted clay.
A jewel in a ten-times-barred-up chest
Is a bold spirit in a loyal breast.
Mine honor is my life, both grow in one;
Take honor from me, and my life is done.
184   Then, dear my liege, mine honor let me try;
In that I live, and for that will I die.

KING
186   Cousin, throw up your gage. Do you begin.

BOLINGBROKE
O, God defend my soul from such deep sin!
Shall I seem crestfallen in my father's sight?
189   Or with pale beggar-fear impeach my height
190   Before this outdared dastard? Ere my tongue
191   Shall wound my honor with such feeble wrong
192   Or sound so base a parle, my teeth shall tear
193   The slavish motive of recanting fear
194   And spit it bleeding in his high disgrace,
Where shame doth harbor, even in Mowbray's face.
                                        [Exit Gaunt.]

KING
We were not born to sue, but to command;
Which since we cannot do to make you friends,
Be ready, as your lives shall answer it,

---

174 *Lions . . . leopards* i.e. kings . . . nobles   184 *try* put to trial   186 *throw
up* (possibly to the king on his high seat)   189 *impeach my height* dishonor
my high rank   190 *outdared* intimidated; *dastard* coward   191 *feeble
wrong* injury only a weak man would submit to   192 *parle* parley, truce
193 *motive* moving part, here his tongue   194 *in* to

At Coventry upon Saint Lambert's day.   199
There shall your swords and lances arbitrate
The swelling difference of your settled hate.
Since we cannot atone you, we shall see   202
Justice design the victor's chivalry.   203
Lord Marshal, command our officers-at-arms
Be ready to direct these home alarms.   205

                       Exit [with others].

*

Enter John of Gaunt with the Duchess of Gloucester.   I, ii

GAUNT

Alas, the part I had in Woodstock's blood   1
Doth more solicit me than your exclaims
To stir against the butchers of his life!
But since correction lieth in those hands   4
Which made the fault that we cannot correct,
Put we our quarrel to the will of heaven,
Who, when they see the hours ripe on earth,
Will rain hot vengeance on offenders' heads.

DUCHESS

Finds brotherhood in thee no sharper spur?
Hath love in thy old blood no living fire?
Edward's seven sons, whereof thyself art one,   11
Were as seven vials of his sacred blood,
Or seven fair branches springing from one root.
Some of those seven are dried by nature's course,
Some of those branches by the Destinies cut;
But Thomas, my dear lord, my life, my Gloucester,

---

199 *Saint Lambert's day* September 17   202 *atone* reconcile   203 *Justice*
... *chivalry* justice point out the true knight by giving him the victory   205
home alarms troubles in England as distinct from the Irish war
I, ii Within a residence of the Duke of Lancaster   1 *the part ... blood* my
being his brother; *Woodstock* (the Duke of Gloucester's name was Thomas
of Woodstock)   4 *those hands* i.e. Richard's   11 *Edward* Edward III

One vial full of Edward's sacred blood,
One flourishing branch of his most royal root,
Is cracked, and all the precious liquor spilt,
Is hacked down, and his summer leaves all faded,
21 By envy's hand and murder's bloody axe.
Ah, Gaunt, his blood was thine! That bed, that womb,
23 That metal, that self mould that fashioned thee,
Made him a man; and though thou livest and breathest,
Yet art thou slain in him. Thou dost consent
In some large measure to thy father's death
In that thou seest thy wretched brother die,
28 Who was the model of thy father's life.
Call it not patience, Gaunt; it is despair.
30 In suff'ring thus thy brother to be slaught'red
31 Thou showest the naked pathway to thy life,
Teaching stern murder how to butcher thee.
That which in mean men we entitle patience
Is pale cold cowardice in noble breasts.
What shall I say? To safeguard thine own life
The best way is to venge my Gloucester's death.

GAUNT
37 God's is the quarrel; for God's substitute,
His deputy anointed in his sight,
Hath caused his death; the which if wrongfully,
Let heaven revenge; for I may never lift
An angry arm against his minister.

DUCHESS
Where then, alas, may I complain myself?

GAUNT
To God, the widow's champion and defense.

DUCHESS
Why then, I will. Farewell, old Gaunt.
Thou goest to Coventry, there to behold

---

21 *envy* malicious enmity   23 *self* selfsame   28 *model* image   30 *suff'ring*
permitting   31 *the naked pathway* the path to be open   37 *God's substitute*
the king by divine right

Our cousin Hereford and fell Mowbray fight.   46
O, sit my husband's wrongs on Hereford's spear,
That it may enter butcher Mowbray's breast!
Or, if misfortune miss the first career,   49
Be Mowbray's sins so heavy in his bosom
That they may break his foaming courser's back
And throw the rider headlong in the lists,
A caitiff recreant to my cousin Hereford!   53
Farewell, old Gaunt. Thy sometimes brother's wife   54
With her companion, Grief, must end her life.

GAUNT
Sister, farewell; I must to Coventry.
As much good stay with thee as go with me!

DUCHESS
Yet one word more! Grief boundeth where it falls,
Not with the empty hollowness, but weight.
I take my leave before I have begun,
For sorrow ends not when it seemeth done.
Commend me to thy brother, Edmund York.
Lo, this is all. Nay, yet depart not so!
Though this be all, do not so quickly go.
I shall remember more. Bid him – ah, what? –
With all good speed at Plashy visit me.   66
Alack, and what shall good old York there see
But empty lodgings and unfurnished walls,   68
Unpeopled offices, untrodden stones?   69
And what hear there for welcome but my groans?
Therefore commend me – let him not come there
To seek out sorrow that dwells everywhere.
Desolate, desolate will I hence and die!
The last leave of thee takes my weeping eye.   *Exeunt.*

*

46 *cousin* kinsman   49 *career* charge   53 *caitiff* captive   54 *sometimes* 'late'
66 *Plashy* Gloucester's country seat, in Essex   68 *unfurnished walls* rooms
bare of furniture and hangings   69 *offices* workrooms

I, iii   *Enter Lord Marshal and the Duke Aumerle.*

MARSHAL
My Lord Aumerle, is Harry Hereford armed?

AUMERLE
Yea, at all points, and longs to enter in.

MARSHAL
3   The Duke of Norfolk, sprightfully and bold,
Stays but the summons of the appellant's trumpet.

AUMERLE
Why, then the champions are prepared, and stay
6   For nothing but his majesty's approach.

> *The trumpets sound and the King enters with his*
> *Nobles [, Gaunt, Bushy, Bagot, Green, and others].*
> *When they are set, enter [Mowbray,] the Duke of*
> *Norfolk, in arms, defendant [, and Herald].*

KING
Marshal, demand of yonder champion
The cause of his arrival here in arms.
Ask him his name and orderly proceed
To swear him in the justice of his cause.

MARSHAL
In God's name and the king's, say who thou art,
And why thou comest thus knightly clad in arms;
Against what man thou com'st, and what thy quarrel.
Speak truly on thy knighthood and thy oath,
As so defend thee heaven and thy valor!

MOWBRAY
My name is Thomas Mowbray, Duke of Norfolk,
Who hither come engagèd by my oath
18   (Which God defend a knight should violate!)
Both to defend my loyalty and truth
To God, my king, and my succeeding issue
Against the Duke of Hereford that appeals me;
And, by the grace of God and this mine arm,

I, iii The lists at Coventry   **s.d.** *Aumerle* (as High Constable of England)
3 *sprightfully and bold* with spirit and boldly   **6 s.d.** *defendant* the chal-
lenged   **18** *defend* forbid

To prove him, in defending of myself,
A traitor to my God, my king, and me ;
And as I truly fight, defend me heaven !
    The trumpets sound. Enter [Bolingbroke,] Duke of
    Hereford, appellant, in armor [and Herald].

KING

Marshal, ask yonder knight in arms
Both who he is and why he cometh hither
Thus plated in habiliments of war ;   28
And formally, according to our law,
Depose him in the justice of his cause.   30

MARSHAL

What is thy name ? and wherefore com'st thou hither,
Before King Richard in his royal lists ?
Against whom comest thou ? and what's thy quarrel ?
Speak like a true knight, so defend thee heaven !

BOLINGBROKE

Harry of Hereford, Lancaster, and Derby
Am I, who ready here do stand in arms
To prove, by God's grace and my body's valor
In lists on Thomas Mowbray, Duke of Norfolk,
That he is a traitor foul and dangerous
To God of heaven, King Richard, and to me ;
And as I truly fight, defend me heaven !

MARSHAL

On pain of death, no person be so bold
Or daring-hardy as to touch the lists,
Except the Marshal and such officers
Appointed to direct these fair designs.   45

BOLINGBROKE

Lord Marshal, let me kiss my sovereign's hand
And bow my knee before his majesty ;
For Mowbray and myself are like two men
That vow a long and weary pilgrimage.

---

28 *plated* armored   **30** *Depose him* take his sworn deposition   **45** *direct . . .*
designs conduct this combat fairly

Then let us take a ceremonious leave
And loving farewell of our several friends.

MARSHAL

The appellant in all duty greets your highness
And craves to kiss your hand and take his leave.

KING

We will descend and fold him in our arms.
Cousin of Hereford, as thy cause is right,
So be thy fortune in this royal fight!
Farewell, my blood; which if to-day thou shed,
Lament we may, but not revenge thee dead.

BOLINGBROKE

59 O, let no noble eye profane a tear
For me, if I be gored with Mowbray's spear.
As confident as is the falcon's flight
Against a bird, do I with Mowbray fight.
My loving lord, I take my leave of you;
Of you, my noble cousin, Lord Aumerle;
Not sick, although I have to do with death,
66 But lusty, young, and cheerly drawing breath.
67 Lo, as at English feasts, so I regreet
The daintiest last, to make the end most sweet.
O thou, the earthly author of my blood,
Whose youthful spirit, in me regenerate,
Doth with a twofold vigor lift me up
To reach at victory above my head,
73 Add proof unto mine armor with thy prayers,
And with thy blessings steel my lance's point,
75 That it may enter Mowbray's waxen coat
76 And furbish new the name of John a Gaunt
Even in the lusty havior of his son.

GAUNT

God in thy good cause make thee prosperous!
Be swift like lightning in the execution

---

59 *profane* (because Bolingbroke's defeat would mean that he was a traitor)
66 *cheerly* cheerily   67 *regreet* greet   73 *proof* invulnerability   75 *enter
...coat* pierce his armor as though it were wax   76 *a* of

And let thy blows, doubly redoublèd,
Fall like amazing thunder on the casque   81
Of thy adverse pernicious enemy.
Rouse up thy youthful blood ; be valiant and live.

BOLINGBROKE
Mine innocence and Saint George to thrive !   84

MOWBRAY
However God or fortune cast my lot,
There lives or dies, true to King Richard's throne,
A loyal, just, and upright gentleman.
Never did captive with a freer heart   88
Cast off his chains of bondage and embrace
His golden uncontrolled enfranchisement,
More than my dancing soul doth celebrate
This feast of battle with mine adversary.
Most mighty liege, and my companion peers,
Take from my mouth the wish of happy years.
As gentle and as jocund as to jest   95
Go I to fight. Truth hath a quiet breast.

KING
Farewell, my lord. Securely I espy   97
Virtue with valor couchèd in thine eye.   98
Order the trial, Marshal, and begin.

MARSHAL
Harry of Hereford, Lancaster, and Derby,
Receive thy lance, and God defend the right !

BOLINGBROKE
Strong as a tower in hope, I cry amen.

MARSHAL [to an Officer]
Go bear this lance to Thomas, Duke of Norfolk.

[I.] HERALD
Harry of Hereford, Lancaster, and Derby
Stands here for God, his sovereign, and himself,
On pain to be found false and recreant,

---

81 *amazing* stupefying; *casque* helmet   84 *to thrive* I rely for success on   88
freer more willing   95 *gentle* tranquil; *jest* mock-fight   97 *Securely I espy*
I am confident that I see   98 *couchèd* expressed

To prove the Duke of Norfolk, Thomas Mowbray,
A traitor to his God, his king, and him,
And dares him to set forward to the fight.

2 . HERALD

Here standeth Thomas Mowbray, Duke of Norfolk,
On pain to be found false and recreant,
112   Both to defend himself and to approve
Henry of Hereford, Lancaster, and Derby
To God, his sovereign, and to him disloyal,
Courageously and with a free desire
116   Attending but the signal to begin.

MARSHAL

Sound trumpets, and set forward combatants.
     [A charge sounded.]
118   Stay! The king hath thrown his warder down.

KING

Let them lay by their helmets and their spears
And both return back to their chairs again.
Withdraw with us; and let the trumpets sound
122   While we return these dukes what we decree.
     [A long flourish.]
Draw near,
124   And list what with our council we have done.
For that our kingdom's earth should not be soiled
With that dear blood which it hath fosterèd;
And for our eyes do hate the dire aspect
Of civil wounds ploughed up with neighbors' sword;
And for we think the eagle-wingèd pride
Of sky-aspiring and ambitious thoughts
131   With rival-hating envy set on you
To wake our peace, which in our country's cradle
Draws the sweet infant breath of gentle sleep;
Which so roused up with boist'rous untuned drums,
With harsh-resounding trumpets' dreadful bray

112 *approve* prove 116 *Attending* awaiting 118 *warder* gilded wand
(held by Richard as commander of the trial) 122 *While* until; **s.d.** *flourish*
trumpet-call 124 *list* listen to 131 *set on you* set you on

And grating shock of wrathful iron arms,
Might from our quiet confines fright fair peace
And make us wade even in our kinred's blood:
Therefore we banish you our territories.
You, cousin Hereford, upon pain of life,
Till twice five summers have enriched our fields
Shall not regreet our fair dominions   142
But tread the stranger paths of banishment.   143

BOLINGBROKE
Your will be done. This must my comfort be –
That sun that warms you here shall shine on me,
And those his golden beams to you here lent
Shall point on me and gild my banishment.

KING
Norfolk, for thee remains a heavier doom,
Which I with some unwillingness pronounce:
The sly slow hours shall not determinate   150
The dateless limit of thy dear exile.   151
The hopeless word of 'never to return'
Breathe I against thee, upon pain of life.

MOWBRAY
A heavy sentence, my most sovereign liege,
And all unlooked for from your highness' mouth.
A dearer merit, not so deep a maim   156
As to be cast forth in the common air,
Have I deservèd at your highness' hands.
The language I have learnt these forty years,
My native English, now I must forgo;
And now my tongue's use is to me no more
Than an unstringèd viol or a harp,
Or like a cunning instrument cased up   163
Or, being open, put into his hands   164
That knows no touch to tune the harmony.

142 *regreet* greet again 143 *stranger* alien 150 *determinate* end 151
dateless unlimited; *limit* term; *dear* bitter 156 *dearer* more welcome;
merit reward; *maim* crippling injury 163 *cunning* skillfully made 164
open out of its case

Within my mouth you have enjailed my tongue,
167 Doubly portcullised with my teeth and lips;
And dull, unfeeling, barren ignorance
Is made my jailer to attend on me.
I am too old to fawn upon a nurse,
Too far in years to be a pupil now.
What is thy sentence then but speechless death,
173 Which robs my tongue from breathing native breath?

KING
174 It boots thee not to be compassionate.
175 After our sentence plaining comes too late.

MOWBRAY
Then thus I turn me from my country's light
To dwell in solemn shades of endless night.

KING
Return again and take an oath with thee.
179 Lay on our royal sword your banished hands;
Swear by the duty that you owe to God
(Our part therein we banish with yourselves)
To keep the oath that we administer:
You never shall, so help you truth and God,
Embrace each other's love in banishment;
Nor never look upon each other's face;
Nor never write, regreet, nor reconcile
187 This low'ring tempest of your home-bred hate;
188 Nor never by advisèd purpose meet
To plot, contrive, or complot any ill
'Gainst us, our state, our subjects, or our land.

BOLINGBROKE
I swear.

MOWBRAY
And I, to keep all this.

---

167 *portcullised* enclosed by a movable grating   173 *Which* thy sentence,
which; *breath* speech   174 *boots* helps; *compassionate* sorrowfully lament-
ing   175 *plaining* complaining   179 *Lay . . . hands* (he addresses both
combatants)   187 *low'ring* threatening   188 *advisèd* concerted

BOLINGBROKE

Norfolk, so far as to mine enemy :   193
By this time, had the king permitted us,
One of our souls had wand'red in the air,
Banished this frail sepulchre of our flesh,
As now our flesh is banished from this land.
Confess thy treasons ere thou fly the realm.
Since thou hast far to go, bear not along
The clogging burden of a guilty soul.

MOWBRAY

No, Bolingbroke. If ever I were traitor,
My name be blotted from the book of life
And I from heaven banished as from hence !
But what thou art, God, thou, and I do know ;
And all too soon, I fear, the king shall rue.
Farewell, my liege. Now no way can I stray.
Save back to England, all the world's my way.   *Exit.*

KING

Uncle, even in the glasses of thine eyes   208
I see thy grievèd heart. Thy sad aspect
Hath from the number of his banished years
Plucked four away.
    [To Bolingbroke]
                    Six frozen winters spent,
Return with welcome home from banishment.

BOLINGBROKE

How long a time lies in one little word !
Four lagging winters and four wanton springs   214
End in a word, such is the breath of kings.

GAUNT

I thank my liege that in regard of me
He shortens four years of my son's exile.
But little vantage shall I reap thereby ;
For ere the six years that he hath to spend

---

193 *so . . . enemy* so far as I may speak to my sworn enemy   208 *glasses . . .
eyes* your eyes as mirrors   214 *wanton* luxuriant

Can change their moons and bring their times about,
My oil-dried lamp and time-bewasted light
Shall be extinct with age and endless night,
My inch of taper will be burnt and done,
224   And blindfold death not let me see my son.

KING

Why, uncle, thou hast many years to live.

GAUNT

But not a minute, king, that thou canst give.
Shorten my days thou canst with sullen sorrow
And pluck nights from me, but not lend a morrow.
Thou canst help time to furrow me with age,
230   But stop no wrinkle in his pilgrimage.
231   Thy word is current with him for my death,
But dead, thy kingdom cannot buy my breath.

KING

Thy son is banished upon good advice,
234   Whereto thy tongue a party-verdict gave.
Why at our justice seem'st thou then to low'r?

GAUNT

Things sweet to taste prove in digestion sour.
You urged me as a judge; but I had rather
You would have bid me argue like a father.
O, had it been a stranger, not my child,
240   To smooth his fault I should have been more mild.
241   A partial slander sought I to avoid,
And in the sentence my own life destroyed.
Alas, I looked when some of you should say
I was too strict to make mine own away;
But you gave leave to my unwilling tongue
246   Against my will to do myself this wrong.

KING

Cousin, farewell; and, uncle, bid him so.

---

224 *blindfold death* death, like a blindfold   230 *stop . . . pilgrimage* prevent
no wrinkle that time's course brings   231 *current* valid   234 *party-
verdict* part of the verdict   240 *smooth* gloss over   241 *partial slander*
slander of partiality to my own son.   246 *wrong* injury

Six years we banish him, and he shall go.
[Flourish.] Exit [King with his Train].

AUMERLE
Cousin, farewell. What presence must not know,   249
From where you do remain let paper show.

MARSHAL
My lord, no leave take I; for I will ride,
As far as land will let me, by your side.

GAUNT
O, to what purpose dost thou hoard thy words
That thou returnest no greeting to thy friends?

BOLINGBROKE
I have too few to take my leave of you,
When the tongue's office should be prodigal
To breathe the abundant dolor of the heart.

GAUNT
Thy grief is but thy absence for a time.

BOLINGBROKE
Joy absent, grief is present for that time.

GAUNT
What is six winters? They are quickly gone.

BOLINGBROKE
To men in joy; but grief makes one hour ten.

GAUNT
Call it a travel that thou tak'st for pleasure.

BOLINGBROKE
My heart will sigh when I miscall it so,
Which finds it an enforcèd pilgrimage.

GAUNT
The sullen passage of thy weary steps
Esteem as foil wherein thou art to set   266
The precious jewel of thy home return.

BOLINGBROKE
Nay, rather every tedious stride I make
Will but remember me what a deal of world   269

249 *What . . . know* what you can't say here   **266** *foil* thin, bright metal leaf
placed under a gem to give it additional brilliance   **269** *remember* remind

47

I wander from the jewels that I love.
Must I not serve a long apprenticehood
272   To foreign passages and, in the end,
Having my freedom, boast of nothing else
274   But that I was a journeyman to grief?

GAUNT

All places that the eye of heaven visits
Are to a wise man ports and happy havens.
Teach thy necessity to reason thus:
278   There is no virtue like necessity.
Think not the king did banish thee,
But thou the king. Woe doth the heavier sit
281   Where it perceives it is but faintly borne.
Go, say I sent thee forth to purchase honor,
And not, the king exiled thee; or suppose
Devouring pestilence hangs in our air
And thou art flying to a fresher clime.
286   Look what thy soul holds dear, imagine it
To lie that way thou goest, not whence thou com'st.
Suppose the singing birds musicians,
289   The grass whereon thou tread'st the presence strewed,
The flowers fair ladies, and thy steps no more
291   Than a delightful measure or a dance;
292   For gnarling sorrow hath less power to bite
The man that mocks at it and sets it light.

BOLINGBROKE

O, who can hold a fire in his hand
By thinking on the frosty Caucasus?
Or cloy the hungry edge of appetite
By bare imagination of a feast?
Or wallow naked in December snow
299   By thinking on fantastic summer's heat?

---

272 *foreign passages* experiences abroad   274 *journeyman* worker for a daily
wage, often itinerant   278 *necessity* patiently enduring the inevitable   281
faintly faint-heartedly   286 *Look what* whatever   289 *presence* royal
audience chamber; *strewed* i.e. the floor covered with rushes   291 *measure*
slow, formal dance   292 *gnarling* snarling   299 *fantastic* imaginary

O, no! The apprehension of the good
Gives but the greater feeling to the worse.
Fell sorrow's tooth doth never rankle more   302
Than when he bites, but lanceth not the sore.

GAUNT
Come, come, my son, I'll bring thee on thy way.
Had I thy youth and cause, I would not stay.

BOLINGBROKE
Then, England's ground, farewell; sweet soil, adieu,
My mother, and my nurse, that bears me yet!
Where'er I wander, boast of this I can,
Though banished, yet a true-born English man.
                                        Exeunt.

*

Enter the King, with Green, &c. [Bagot], at one   I, iv
door, and the Lord Aumerle at another.

KING
We did observe. Cousin Aumerle,
How far brought you high Hereford on his way?

AUMERLE
I brought high Hereford, if you call him so,
But to the next high way, and there I left him.

KING
And say, what store of parting tears were shed?

AUMERLE
Faith, none for me; except the northeast wind,   6
Which then blew bitterly against our faces,
Awaked the sleeping rheum, and so by chance   8
Did grace our hollow parting with a tear.   9

KING
What said our cousin when you parted with him?

AUMERLE
'Farewell!'

302 *rankle* inflict a painful, festering wound
I, iv The court of King Richard   6 *for me* for my part   8 *rheum* moisture,
tears   9 *hollow* insincere

49

And, for my heart disdainèd that my tongue
Should so profane the word, that taught me craft
To counterfeit oppression of such grief
That words seemed buried in my sorrow's grave.

16   Marry, would the word 'farewell' have length'ned hours
And added years to his short banishment,
He should have had a volume of farewells;
But since it would not, he had none of me.

KING

20   He is our cousin, cousin; but 'tis doubt,
When time shall call him home from banishment,
22   Whether our kinsman come to see his friends.
Ourself and Bushy, Bagot here, and Green
Observed his courtship to the common people;
How he did seem to dive into their hearts
With humble and familiar courtesy;
What reverence he did throw away on slaves,
Wooing poor craftsmen with the craft of smiles
29   And patient underbearing of his fortune,
30   As 'twere to banish their affects with him.
Off goes his bonnet to an oyster-wench;
A brace of draymen bid God speed him well
And had the tribute of his supple knee,
With 'Thanks, my countrymen, my loving friends';
35   As were our England in reversion his,
And he our subjects' next degree in hope.

GREEN

Well, he is gone, and with him go these thoughts!
38   Now for the rebels which stand out in Ireland,
39   Expedient manage must be made, my liege,
Ere further leisure yield them further means
For their advantage and your highness' loss.

---

16 *Marry* indeed   **20** *'tis* there is   **22** *his friends* us of his own rank   **29** *underbearing* enduring   **30** *affects* affections   **35** *in reversion* by right of legal succession   **38** *stand out* resist   **39** *Expedient* speedy; *manage* plans for controlling

KING
> We will ourself in person to this war ;
> And, for our coffers, with too great a court   43
> And liberal largess, are grown somewhat light,   44
> We are enforced to farm our royal realm,   45
> The revenue whereof shall furnish us
> For our affairs in hand. If that come short,
> Our substitutes at home shall have blank charters,   48
> Whereto, when they shall know what men are rich,
> They shall subscribe them for large sums of gold   50
> And send them after to supply our wants,
> For we will make for Ireland presently.   52
> > *Enter Bushy.*
> Bushy, what news ?

BUSHY
> Old John of Gaunt is grievous sick, my lord,
> Suddenly taken, and hath sent posthaste
> To entreat your majesty to visit him.

KING
> Where lies he ?

BUSHY
> At Ely House.   58

KING
> Now put it, God, in the physician's mind
> To help him to his grave immediately !
> The lining of his coffers shall make coats   61
> To deck our soldiers for these Irish wars.
> Come, gentlemen, let's all go visit him.
> Pray God we may make haste, and come too late !

[ALL]
> Amen.   *Exeunt.*

*

43 *for* because; *too . . . court* too many courtiers (Richard's extravagance was notorious) 44 *largess* gifts 45 *farm* lease (the authority to collect taxes was deputed in exchange for cash in hand) 48 *blank charters* in effect, loans to the crown on which the amount was filled in by the king's agents 50 *subscribe* put them down 52 *presently* at once 58 *Ely House* the Bishop of Ely's palace in London 61 *coats* coats of mail

II, i   *Enter John of Gaunt, sick, with the Duke of York, &c.*

GAUNT
Will the king come, that I may breathe my last
In wholesome counsel to his unstaid youth?

YORK
Vex not yourself nor strive not with your breath,
For all in vain comes counsel to his ear.

GAUNT
O, but they say the tongues of dying men
Enforce attention like deep harmony.
Where words are scarce, they are seldom spent in vain,
For they breathe truth that breathe their words in pain.
He that no more must say is listened more
10   Than they whom youth and ease have taught to glose.
11 More are men's ends marked than their lives before.
    The setting sun, and music at the close,
13 As the last taste of sweets, is sweetest last,
    Writ in remembrance more than things long past.
15 Though Richard my life's counsel would not hear,
16 My death's sad tale may yet undeaf his ear.

YORK
No; it is stopped with other, flattering sounds,
18 As praises, of whose taste the wise are fond,
19 Lascivious metres, to whose venom sound
    The open ear of youth doth always listen;
    Report of fashions in proud Italy,
22 Whose manners still our tardy apish nation
    Limps after in base imitation.
    Where doth the world thrust forth a vanity
25 (So it be new, there's no respect how vile)
    That is not quickly buzzed into his ears?

II, i Within Ely House   **10** *glose* speak empty words in flattery   **11** *marked* heeded   **13** *is sweetest last* lingers longest in memory   **15** *life's* lifelong **16** *My . . . tale* my serious dying words   **18** *of . . . fond* which even the wise are too fond of   **19** *venom* poisonous   **22** *still* always; *tardy apish* aping foreign fashions after they have become stale   **25** *there's no respect* no one considers

Then all too late comes counsel to be heard
Where will doth mutiny with wit's regard.   28
Direct not him whose way himself will choose.
'Tis breath thou lack'st, and that breath wilt thou lose.

GAUNT
Methinks I am a prophet new inspired
And thus, expiring, do foretell of him :
His rash fierce blaze of riot cannot last,
For violent fires soon burn out themselves ;
Small show'rs last long, but sudden storms are short ;
He tires betimes that spurs too fast betimes ;   36
With eager feeding food doth choke the feeder ;
Light vanity, insatiate cormorant,   38
Consuming means, soon preys upon itself.
This royal throne of kings, this scept'red isle,
This earth of majesty, this seat of Mars,
This other Eden, demi-paradise,
This fortress built by Nature for herself
Against infection and the hand of war,   44
This happy breed of men, this little world,
This precious stone set in the silver sea,
Which serves it in the office of a wall,
Or as a moat defensive to a house,
Against the envy of less happier lands ;
This blessed plot, this earth, this realm, this England,
This nurse, this teeming womb of royal kings,
Feared by their breed and famous by their birth,   52
Renownèd for their deeds as far from home,
For Christian service and true chivalry,
As is the sepulchre in stubborn Jewry   55
Of the world's ransom, blessed Mary's son ;
This land of such dear souls, this dear dear land,
Dear for her reputation through the world,

28 *will* natural inclination; *wit's regard* what reason esteems   36 *betimes*
early   38 *cormorant* glutton   44 *infection* plague and moral contamination
52 *breed* ancestral reputation for valor   55 *stubborn* obstinate in rejecting
Christ and resisting the Crusaders

53

Is now leased out (I die pronouncing it)
60   Like to a tenement or pelting farm.
England, bound in with the triumphant sea,
Whose rocky shore beats back the envious siege
Of wat'ry Neptune, is now bound in with shame,
64   With inky blots and rotten parchment bonds.
That England that was wont to conquer others
Hath made a shameful conquest of itself.
Ah, would the scandal vanish with my life,
How happy then were my ensuing death!

YORK

The king is come. Deal mildly with his youth;
70   For young hot colts, being raged, do rage the more.

Enter King and Queen, & c. [Aumerle, Bushy, Green,
Bagot, Ross, and Willoughby].

QUEEN

How fares our noble uncle Lancaster?

KING

What comfort, man? How is't with aged Gaunt?

GAUNT

73   O, how that name befits my composition!
Old Gaunt indeed, and gaunt in being old.
Within me grief hath kept a tedious fast;
And who abstains from meat that is not gaunt?
77   For sleeping England long time have I watched;
Watching breeds leanness, leanness is all gaunt.
The pleasure that some fathers feed upon
Is my strict fast – I mean my children's looks –
And therein fasting hast thou made me gaunt.
Gaunt am I for the grave, gaunt as a grave,
83   Whose hollow womb inherits naught but bones.

KING

84   Can sick men play so nicely with their names?

---

60 *tenement* rented land or building; *pelting* paltry   64 *blots* i.e. the blank
charters   70 *raged* enraged   73 *composition* body and mind   77 *watched*
stayed awake at night   83 *inherits* will get   84 *so nicely* making such fine
puns (Richard is ironical)

GAUNT
> No, misery makes sport to mock itself.   85
> Since thou dost seek to kill my name in me,
> I mock my name, great king, to flatter thee.

KING
> Should dying men flatter with those that live?   88

GAUNT
> No, no! men living flatter those that die.

KING
> Thou, now a-dying, sayest thou flatterest me.

GAUNT
> O, no! thou diest, though I the sicker be.

KING
> I am in health, I breathe, and see thee ill.

GAUNT
> Now, he that made me knows I see thee ill;
> Ill in myself to see, and in thee seeing ill.
> Thy deathbed is no lesser than thy land,
> Wherein thou liest in reputation sick;
> And thou, too careless patient as thou art,
> Committ'st thy anointed body to the cure
> Of those physicians that first wounded thee.
> A thousand flatterers sit within thy crown,
> Whose compass is no bigger than thy head;
> And yet, incagèd in so small a verge,   102
> The waste is no whit lesser than thy land.
> O, had thy grandsire, with a prophet's eye,
> Seen how his son's son should destroy his sons,
> From forth thy reach he would have laid thy shame,
> Deposing thee before thou wert possessed,   107
> Which art possessed now to depose thyself.
> Why, cousin, wert thou regent of the world,
> It were a shame to let this land by lease;
> But, for thy world enjoying but this land,

85 *to mock* of mocking   88 *flatter with* seek to please   102 *verge* compass
107–08 *possessed* . . . *possessed* put in possession . . . possessed of a devil

Is it not more than shame to shame it so ?

113 Landlord of England art thou now, not king.

114 Thy state of law is bondslave to the law,
And thou –

KING   A lunatic lean-witted fool,

116 Presuming on an ague's privilege,

117 Darest with thy frozen admonition
Make pale our cheek, chasing the royal blood

119 With fury from his native residence.
Now, by my seat's right royal majesty,
Wert thou not brother to great Edward's son,

122 This tongue that runs so roundly in thy head
Should run thy head from thy unreverent shoulders.

GAUNT

O, spare me not, my brother Edward's son,
For that I was his father Edward's son !

126 That blood already, like the pelican,
Hast thou tapped out and drunkenly caroused.
My brother Gloucester, plain well-meaning soul –

129 Whom fair befall in heaven 'mongst happy souls ! –

130 May be a precedent and witness good
That thou respect'st not spilling Edward's blood.
Join with the present sickness that I have,

133 And thy unkindness be like crooked age,
To crop at once a too-long-withered flower.
Live in thy shame, but die not shame with thee !
These words hereafter thy tormenters be !
Convey me to my bed, then to my grave.
Love they to live that love and honor have.

                    Exit [borne off by Attendants].

---

113 *Landlord* one who leases out a property **114** *Thy . . . to the law* your legal status is that of subject, not king **116** *ague's privilege* a not-too-ill man's privilege to be cross **117** *frozen* chilly – cold and caused by a chill **119** *his* its **122** *roundly* freely and bluntly **126** *pelican* (believed to feed its young with its own blood) **129** *fair befall* may good befall **130** *precedent* token **133** *crooked* bent like a sickle

KING

And let them die that age and sullens have;   139
For both hast thou, and both become the grave.

YORK

I do beseech your majesty impute his words
To wayward sickliness and age in him.
He loves you, on my life, and holds you dear
As Harry Duke of Hereford, were he here.

KING

Right, you say true! As Hereford's love, so his;   145
As theirs, so mine; and all be as it is!
      [Enter Northumberland.]

NORTHUMBERLAND

My liege, old Gaunt commends him to your majesty.

KING

What says he?

NORTHUMBERLAND Nay, nothing; all is said.
His tongue is now a stringless instrument;
Words, life, and all, old Lancaster hath spent.

YORK

Be York the next that must be bankrout so!   151
Though death be poor, it ends a mortal woe.

KING

The ripest fruit first falls, and so doth he;
His time is spent, our pilgrimage must be.   154
So much for that. Now for our Irish wars.
We must supplant those rough rug-headed kerns,   156
Which live like venom where no venom else   157
But only they have privilege to live.
And, for these great affairs do ask some charge,   159
Towards our assistance we do seize to us
The plate, coin, revenues, and moveables
Whereof our uncle Gaunt did stand possessed.

---

139 *sullens* sulks   145 *Right . . . his* (the KING purposely takes the opposite of York's meaning)   151 *bankrout* bankrupt   154 *must be* is yet to be finished   156 *rug-headed* shaggy-haired; *kerns* light-armed footsoldiers   157 *venom* poisonous snakes   159 *charge* outlay

YORK

How long shall I be patient? Ah, how long
Shall tender duty make me suffer wrong?
Not Gloucester's death, nor Hereford's banishment,
166 Nor Gaunt's rebukes, nor England's private wrongs,
167 Nor the prevention of poor Bolingbroke
About his marriage, nor my own disgrace,
Have ever made me sour my patient cheek
Or bend one wrinkle on my sovereign's face.
I am the last of noble Edward's sons,
Of whom thy father, Prince of Wales, was first.
In war was never lion raged more fierce,
In peace was never gentle lamb more mild,
Than was that young and princely gentleman.
His face thou hast, for even so looked he,
177 Accomplished with the number of thy hours;
But when he frowned, it was against the French
And not against his friends. His noble hand
Did win what he did spend, and spent not that
Which his triumphant father's hand had won.
His hands were guilty of no kinred blood,
But bloody with the enemies of his kin.
O Richard! York is too far gone with grief,
185 Or else he never would compare between.

KING

Why, uncle, what's the matter?

YORK   O my liege,
Pardon me, if you please; if not, I, pleased
188 Not to be pardoned, am content withal.
Seek you to seize and gripe into your hands
190 The royalties and rights of banished Hereford?
Is not Gaunt dead? and doth not Hereford live?

---

166 *Gaunt's rebukes* reprimands to Gaunt   167–68 *prevention . . . marriage*
(Richard forestalled Bolingbroke's match with the Duc du Berri's daughter)
177 *Accomplished . . . hours* at your age   185 *compare between* make com-
parisons   188 *withal* nonetheless   190 *royalties* rights as a member of the
royal family

Was not Gaunt just ? and is not Harry true ?
Did not the one deserve to have an heir ?
Is not his heir a well-deserving son ?
Take Hereford's rights away, and take from Time
His charters and his customary rights ;   196
Let not to-morrow then ensue to-day ;   197
Be not thyself – for how art thou a king
But by fair sequence and succession ?
Now, afore God (God forbid I say true !)
If you do wrongfully seize Hereford's rights,
Call in the letters patents that he hath   202
By his attorneys general to sue
His livery, and deny his off'red homage,   204
You pluck a thousand dangers on your head,
You lose a thousand well-disposèd hearts,
And prick my tender patience to those thoughts
Which honor and allegiance cannot think.

KING

Think what you will, we seize into our hands
His plate, his goods, his money, and his lands.

YORK

I'll not be by the while. My liege, farewell.
What will ensue hereof there's none can tell ;
But by bad courses may be understood   213
That their events can never fall out good.   *Exit.*   214

KING

Go, Bushy, to the Earl of Wiltshire straight.   215
Bid him repair to us to Ely House
To see this business. To-morrow next   217
We will for Ireland ; and 'tis time, I trow.   218
And we create, in absence of ourself,

---

196 *his customary rights* (one of Time's rights was to bring the heir his inheritance) **197** *ensue* follow **202–04** *letters patents . . . livery* royal grants through legal representatives to sue for possession of his inheritance **204** *homage* avowal of allegiance **213** *by* with respect to **214** *events* outcomes **215** *Earl of Wiltshire* Richard's Lord Treasurer; *straight* at once **217** *see* see to; *To-morrow next* to-morrow **218** *trow* believe

Our uncle York Lord Governor of England;
For he is just and always loved us well.
Come on, our queen. To-morrow must we part.
Be merry, for our time of stay is short.

[Flourish.] Exeunt King and Queen.
Manet Northumberland [with Willoughby and Ross].

NORTHUMBERLAND
Well, lords, the Duke of Lancaster is dead.

ROSS
And living too; for now his son is duke.

WILLOUGHBY
Barely in title, not in revenues.

NORTHUMBERLAND
Richly in both, if justice had her right.

ROSS
228 My heart is great; but it must break with silence,
Ere't be disburdened with a liberal tongue.

NORTHUMBERLAND
Nay, speak thy mind; and let him ne'er speak more
That speaks thy words again to do thee harm!

WILLOUGHBY
232 Tends that thou wouldst speak to the Duke of
       Hereford?
If it be so, out with it boldly, man!
Quick is mine ear to hear of good towards him.

ROSS
No good at all that I can do for him;
Unless you call it good to pity him,
Bereft and gelded of his patrimony.

NORTHUMBERLAND
Now, afore God, 'tis shame such wrongs are borne
239 In him a royal prince and many moe
Of noble blood in this declining land.
The king is not himself, but basely led
By flatterers; and what they will inform,

228 *great* swollen, heavy   232 *Tends ... to* does ... concern   239 *moe* more

Merely in hate, 'gainst any of us all,   243
That will the king severely prosecute   244
'Gainst us, our lives, our children, and our heirs.

ROSS
The commons hath he pilled with grievous taxes   246
And quite lost their hearts; the nobles hath he fined
For ancient quarrels and quite lost their hearts.

WILLOUGHBY
And daily new exactions are devised,
As blanks, benevolences, and I wot not what;   250
But what, a God's name, doth become of this?   251

NORTHUMBERLAND
Wars hath not wasted it, for warred he hath not,
But basely yielded upon compromise
That which his noble ancestors achieved with blows.
More hath he spent in peace than they in wars.

ROSS
The Earl of Wiltshire hath the realm in farm.

WILLOUGHBY
The king's grown bankrout, like a broken man.

NORTHUMBERLAND
Reproach and dissolution hangeth over him.

ROSS
He hath not money for these Irish wars,
His burdenous taxations notwithstanding,
But by the robbing of the banished duke.

NORTHUMBERLAND
His noble kinsman. Most degenerate king!
But, lords, we hear this fearful tempest sing,
Yet seek no shelter to avoid the storm.
We see the wind sit sore upon our sails,   265
And yet we strike not, but securely perish.   266

---

243 *Merely* purely 244 *prosecute* follow up 246 *pilled* skinned 250
blanks blank charters (see I, iv, 48n.); *benevolences* 'voluntary' loans to the
crown; *wot* know 251 *a* in 265 *sit sore* press grievously 266 *strike* lower
sail or strike back; *securely* overconfidently

ROSS
  We see the very wrack that we must suffer,
268 And unavoided is the danger now
  For suffering so the causes of our wrack.

NORTHUMBERLAND
  Not so. Even through the hollow eyes of death
  I spy life peering; but I dare not say
  How near the tidings of our comfort is.

WILLOUGHBY
  Nay, let us share thy thoughts as thou dost ours.

ROSS
  Be confident to speak, Northumberland.
  We three are but thyself, and speaking so,
  Thy words are but as thoughts. Therefore be bold.

NORTHUMBERLAND
  Then thus: I have from Le Port Blanc, a bay
278 In Brittaine, received intelligence
  That Harry Duke of Hereford, Rainold Lord Cobham,
280 [The son and heir of the Earl of Arundel,]
281 That late broke from the Duke of Exeter,
282 His brother, Archbishop late of Canterbury,
  Sir Thomas Erpingham, Sir John Ramston,
  Sir John Norbery, Sir Robert Waterton, and Francis
    Coint,
  All these well furnished by the Duke of Brittaine
286 With eight tall ships, three thousand men of war,
287 Are making hither with all due expedience
  And shortly mean to touch our northern shore.
  Perhaps they had ere this, but that they stay
290 The first departing of the king for Ireland.

---

268 *unavoided* unavoidable   278 *Brittaine* Brittany; *intelligence* information
280 (this line or a similarly worded one was deleted for political reasons;
Elizabeth had imprisoned the son of the then Earl of Arundel)   281 *broke*
escaped   282 *late* until recently (he had been deprived of the office by the
Pope at Richard's request)   286 *tall* fine; *men of war* fighting men   287
expedience speed   290 *The first departing* until after the departure

If then we shall shake off our slavish yoke,
Imp out our drooping country's broken wing,   292
Redeem from broking pawn the blemished crown,   293
Wipe off the dust that hides our sceptre's gilt,   294
And make high majesty look like itself,
Away with me in post to Ravenspurgh;   296
But if you faint, as fearing to do so,   297
Stay and be secret, and myself will go.

ROSS
To horse, to horse! Urge doubts to them that fear.

WILLOUGHBY
Hold out my horse, and I will first be there.   *Exeunt.* 300

*

Enter the Queen, Bushy, Bagot.   II, ii
BUSHY
Madam, your majesty is too much sad.
You promised, when you parted with the king,
To lay aside life-harming heaviness
And entertain a cheerful disposition.

QUEEN
To please the king, I did; to please myself,
I cannot do it. Yet I know no cause
Why I should welcome such a guest as grief
Save bidding farewell to so sweet a guest
As my sweet Richard. Yet again, methinks,
Some unborn sorrow, ripe in fortune's womb,
Is coming towards me, and my inward soul
With nothing trembles. At something it grieves   12
More than with parting from my lord the king.

---

292 *Imp out* graft new feathers on   293 *broking pawn* the possession of the
king's moneylenders   294 *gilt* golden lustre   296 *post* haste; *Ravenspurgh*
a port on the River Humber, now submerged by the sea   297 *faint* are
faint-hearted   300 *Hold . . . and* if my horse holds out
II, ii Within Windsor Castle   12 *With* at

BUSHY

 Each substance of a grief hath twenty shadows,
 Which shows like grief itself, but is not so ;
 For sorrow's eye, glazèd with blinding tears,
 Divides one thing entire to many objects,
18 Like perspectives, which rightly gazed upon,
 Show nothing but confusion – eyed awry,
 Distinguish form. So your sweet majesty,
 Looking awry upon your lord's departure,
 Find shapes of grief more than himself to wail,
 Which, looked on as it is, is naught but shadows
 Of what it is not. Then, thrice-gracious queen,
 More than your lord's departure weep not. More's not
  seen ;
 Or if it be, 'tis with false sorrow's eye,
 Which for things true weeps things imaginary.

QUEEN

 It may be so ; but yet my inward soul
 Persuades me it is otherwise. Howe'er it be,
 I cannot but be sad – so heavy sad
 As, though in thinking on no thought I think,
 Makes me with heavy nothing faint and shrink.

BUSHY

33 'Tis nothing but conceit, my gracious lady.

QUEEN

34 'Tis nothing less. Conceit is still derived
 From some forefather grief. Mine is not so,
 For nothing hath begot my something grief,
37 Or something hath the nothing that I grieve.
38 'Tis in reversion that I do possess ;
 But what it is, that is not yet known – what,
 I cannot name. 'Tis nameless woe, I wot.

---

18 *perspectives* raised pictures or designs which appear only when looked at from the side (*awry*) **33** *conceit* fancy **34** *nothing less* anything but that **37** *something . . . grieve* my causeless grief has something in it **38** *'Tis . . . possess* what I feel is like a property which will devolve upon me later; I can't describe it yet (see I, iv, 35n.)

[Enter Green.]

GREEN

    God save your majesty! and well met, gentlemen.

    I hope the king is not yet shipped for Ireland.

QUEEN

    Why hopest thou so? 'Tis better hope he is;

    For his designs crave haste, his haste good hope.

    Then wherefore dost thou hope he is not shipped?

GREEN

    That he, our hope, might have retired his power   46

    And driven into despair an enemy's hope

    Who strongly hath set footing in this land.   48

    The banished Bolingbroke repeals himself   49

    And with uplifted arms is safe arrived   50

    At Ravenspurgh.

QUEEN   Now God in heaven forbid!

GREEN

    Ah, madam, 'tis too true; and that is worse,   52

    The Lord Northumberland, his son young Henry Percy,

    The Lords of Ross, Beaumond, and Willoughby,

    With all their powerful friends, are fled to him.

BUSHY

    Why have you not proclaimed Northumberland

    And all the rest revolted faction traitors?   57

GREEN

    We have; whereupon the Earl of Worcester

    Hath broken his staff, resigned his stewardship,   59

    And all the household servants fled with him

    To Bolingbroke.

QUEEN

    So, Green, thou art the midwife to my woe,

    And Bolingbroke my sorrow's dismal heir.   63

    Now hath my soul brought forth her prodigy;   64

---

46 *retired* drawn back   **48** *strongly* with strong support   **49** *repeals* recalls
50 *uplifted arms* brandished weapons   **52** *that* what   **57** *revolted . . . traitors*
a rebellious clique of traitors   **59** *staff* (the sign of his office)   **63** *dismal*
ill-omened   **64** *prodigy* monster

And I, a gasping new-delivered mother,
Have woe to woe, sorrow to sorrow joined.

BUSHY
Despair not, madam.

QUEEN   Who shall hinder me?
I will despair, and be at enmity
69   With cozening Hope. He is a flatterer,
A parasite, a keeper-back of Death,
71   Who gently would dissolve the bands of life,
72   Which false Hope lingers in extremity.
        [Enter York.]

GREEN
Here comes the Duke of York.

QUEEN
74   With signs of war about his aged neck.
75   O, full of careful business are his looks.
Uncle, for God's sake, speak comfortable words!

YORK
Should I do so, I should belie my thoughts.
Comfort 's in heaven, and we are on the earth,
79   Where nothing lives but crosses, cares, and grief.
Your husband, he is gone to save far off,
Whilst others come to make him lose at home.
Here am I left to underprop his land,
Who, weak with age, cannot support myself.
84   Now comes the sick hour that his surfeit made;
Now shall he try his friends that flattered him.
        [Enter a Servingman.]

SERVINGMAN
My lord, your son was gone before I came.

YORK
He was? Why, so! Go all which way it will!
The nobles they are fled, the commons they are cold
And will, I fear, revolt on Hereford's side.

---

69 *cozening* deceitful   **71** *bands* bonds   **72** *lingers* causes to linger   **74**
With . . . neck in armor   **75** *careful business* anxious preoccupation   **79**
crosses thwartings   **84** *surfeit* excess

Sirrah, get thee to Plashy to my sister Gloucester ;
Bid her send me presently a thousand pound.
Hold, take my ring.

SERVINGMAN

My lord, I had forgot to tell your lordship
To-day, as I came by, I callèd there –
But I shall grieve you to report the rest.

YORK

What is't, knave ?

SERVINGMAN

An hour before I came the duchess died.

YORK

God for his mercy ! what a tide of woes
Comes rushing on this woeful land at once !
I know not what to do. I would to God
(So my untruth had not provoked him to it)   101
The king had cut off my head with my brother's.
What, are there no posts dispatched for Ireland ?
How shall we do for money for these wars ?
Come, sister – cousin I would say – pray pardon me.
Go, fellow, get thee home, provide some carts
And bring away the armor that is there.

> *[Exit Servingman.]*

Gentlemen, will you go muster men ?
If I know how or which way to order these affairs,
Thus disorderly thrust into my hands,
Never believe me. Both are my kinsmen.
Th' one is my sovereign, whom both my oath
And duty bids defend ; t' other again
Is my kinsman, whom the king hath wronged,
Whom conscience and my kinred bids to right.
Well, somewhat we must do. Come, cousin, I'll
Dispose of you.   117
Gentlemen, go muster up your men,
And meet me presently at Berkeley.

---

101 *untruth* disloyalty   117 *Dispose of* make arrangements for

I should to Plashy too,
But time will not permit. All is uneven,
122 And everything is left at six and seven.

Exeunt Duke, Queen.
Manent Bushy, [Bagot,] Green.

BUSHY
The wind sits fair for news to go for Ireland,
But none returns. For us to levy power
Proportionable to the enemy
Is all unpossible.

GREEN
Besides, our nearness to the king in love
128 Is near the hate of those love not the king.

BAGOT
And that's the wavering commons; for their love
Lies in their purses, and whoso empties them,
By so much fills their hearts with deadly hate.

BUSHY
132 Wherein the king stands generally condemned.

BAGOT
133 If judgment lie in them, then so do we,
Because we ever have been near the king.

GREEN
Well, I will for refuge straight to Bristol Castle.
The Earl of Wiltshire is already there.

BUSHY
137 Thither will I with you; for little office
138 Will the hateful commons perform for us,
Except like curs to tear us all to pieces.
Will you go along with us?

BAGOT
No; I will to Ireland to his majesty.
Farewell. If heart's presages be not vain,
We three here part that ne'er shall meet again.

---

122 *at six and seven* in confusion   128 *those love* those who love   132
Wherein on which grounds   133 *If . . . them* if our doom depends on them
137 *office* service   138 *hateful* angry

BUSHY
  That's as York thrives to beat back Bolingbroke.
GREEN
  Alas, poor duke! The task he undertakes
  Is numb'ring sands and drinking oceans dry.
  Where one on his side fights, thousands will fly.
BAGOT
  Farewell at once – for once, for all, and ever.
BUSHY
  Well, we may meet again.
BAGOT   I fear me, never.   *[Exeunt.]*

*

Enter [Bolingbroke the Duke of] Hereford, [and]   II, iii
    Northumberland.
BOLINGBROKE
  How far is it, my lord, to Berkeley now?
NORTHUMBERLAND
  Believe me, noble lord,
  I am a stranger here in Gloucestershire.
  These high wild hills and rough uneven ways
  Draws out our miles and makes them wearisome;
  And yet your fair discourse hath been as sugar,
  Making the hard way sweet and delectable.
  But I bethink me what a weary way
  From Ravenspurgh to Cotswold will be found
  In Ross and Willoughby, wanting your company,   10
  Which, I protest, hath very much beguiled
  The tediousness and process of my travel;   12
  But theirs is sweet'ned with the hope to have
  The present benefit which I possess;
  And hope to joy is little less in joy

II, iii An open place in Gloucestershire   10 *In* by   12 *tediousness and process* tedious process

16   Than hope enjoyed. By this the weary lords
      Shall make their way seem short, as mine hath done
      By sight of what I have, your noble company.

BOLINGBROKE
      Of much less value is my company
      Than your good words. But who comes here?
            Enter Harry Percy.

NORTHUMBERLAND
      It is my son, young Harry Percy,
22   Sent from my brother Worcester, whencesoever.
      Harry, how fares your uncle?

PERCY
      I had thought, my lord, to have learned his health of
            you.

NORTHUMBERLAND
      Why, is he not with the queen?

PERCY
      No, my good lord; he hath forsook the court,
      Broken his staff of office, and dispersed
      The household of the king.

NORTHUMBERLAND   What was his reason?
      He was not so resolved when last we spake together.

PERCY
30   Because your lordship was proclaimèd traitor.
      But he, my lord, is gone to Ravenspurgh
      To offer service to the Duke of Hereford;
      And sent me over by Berkeley to discover
      What power the Duke of York had levied there;
      Then with directions to repair to Ravenspurgh.

NORTHUMBERLAND
      Have you forgot the Duke of Hereford, boy?

PERCY
      No, my good lord, for that is not forgot
      Which ne'er I did remember. To my knowledge,
      I never in my life did look on him.

16 *this* this expectation   22 *whencesoever* wherever he may be

NORTHUMBERLAND

Then learn to know him now. This is the duke.

PERCY

My gracious lord, I tender you my service,
Such as it is, being tender, raw, and young;　　　　42
Which elder days shall ripen and confirm
To more approvèd service and desert.　　　　44

BOLINGBROKE

I thank thee, gentle Percy; and be sure
I count myself in nothing else so happy
As in a soul rememb'ring my good friends;
And, as my fortune ripens with thy love,
It shall be still thy true love's recompense.
My heart this covenant makes, my hand thus seals it.

NORTHUMBERLAND

How far is it to Berkeley? and what stir
Keeps good old York there with his men of war?

PERCY

There stands the castle by yon tuft of trees,
Manned with three hundred men, as I have heard;
And in it are the Lords of York, Berkeley, and Seymour,
None else of name and noble estimate.
　　[Enter Ross and Willoughby.]

NORTHUMBERLAND

Here come the Lords of Ross and Willoughby,
Bloody with spurring, fiery red with haste.

BOLINGBROKE

Welcome, my lords. I wot your love pursues
A banished traitor. All my treasury
Is yet but unfelt thanks, which, more enriched,　　　　61
Shall be your love and labor's recompense.

ROSS

Your presence makes us rich, most noble lord.

WILLOUGHBY

And far surmounts our labor to attain it.

---

42 *raw* inexperienced　44 *approvèd* demonstrated　61 *unfelt* intangible

BOLINGBROKE

Evermore thanks, the exchequer of the poor,
Which, till my infant fortune comes to years,
Stands for my bounty. But who comes here?
[Enter Berkeley.]

NORTHUMBERLAND

It is my Lord of Berkeley, as I guess.

BERKELEY

My Lord of Hereford, my message is to you.

BOLINGBROKE

My lord, my answer is – 'to Lancaster';
And I am come to seek that name in England;
And I must find that title in your tongue
Before I make reply to aught you say.

BERKELEY

Mistake me not, my lord. 'Tis not my meaning
75 To rase one title of your honor out.
To you, my lord, I come (what lord you will)
From the most gracious regent of this land,
The Duke of York, to know what pricks you on
79 To take advantage of the absent time
80 And fright our native peace with self-borne arms.
[Enter York attended.]

BOLINGBROKE

I shall not need transport my words by you;
Here comes his grace in person. My noble uncle!
[Kneels.]

YORK

Show me thy humble heart, and not thy knee,
84 Whose duty is deceivable and false.

BOLINGBROKE

My gracious uncle!

YORK

Tut, tut!
Grace me no grace, nor uncle me no uncle.

---

75 *rase* erase   79 *absent time* time of the king's absence   80 *self-borne*
begotten and carried by you   84 *duty* i.e. act of kneeling; *deceivable* deceitful

I am no traitor's uncle, and that word 'grace'
In an ungracious mouth is but profane.
Why have those banished and forbidden legs
Dared once to touch a dust of England's ground?   91
But then more why? – why have they dared to march
So many miles upon her peaceful bosom,
Frighting her pale-faced villages with war
And ostentation of despisèd arms?   95
Com'st thou because the anointed king is hence?
Why, foolish boy, the king is left behind,
And in my loyal bosom lies his power.
Were I but now lord of such hot youth
As when brave Gaunt thy father and myself
Rescued the Black Prince, that young Mars of men,
From forth the ranks of many thousand French,
O, then how quickly should this arm of mine,
Now prisoner to the palsy, chastise thee
And minister correction to thy fault!

BOLINGBROKE
My gracious uncle, let me know my fault;
On what condition stands it and wherein?   107
YORK
Even in condition of the worst degree,
In gross rebellion and detested treason.
Thou art a banished man; and here art come,
Before the expiration of thy time,
In braving arms against thy sovereign.   112
BOLINGBROKE
As I was banished, I was banished Hereford;
But as I come, I come for Lancaster.   114
And, noble uncle, I beseech your grace
Look on my wrongs with an indifferent eye.   116
You are my father, for methinks in you

91 *dust* speck   95 *ostentation* display; *despisèd* despicable   107 *On . . . it*
on what defect in me is it based; *wherein* of what does it consist   112
braving defiant   114 *for* as   116 *indifferent* impartial

I see old Gaunt alive. O, then, my father,
Will you permit that I shall stand condemned
A wandering vagabond, my rights and royalties
Plucked from my arms perforce, and given away
122 To upstart unthrifts? Wherefore was I born?
If that my cousin king be King in England,
It must be granted I am Duke of Lancaster.
You have a son, Aumerle, my noble cousin.
126 Had you first died, and he been thus trod down,
He should have found his uncle Gaunt a father
128 To rouse his wrongs and chase them to the bay.
I am denied to sue my livery here,
And yet my letters patents give me leave.
131 My father's goods are all distrained and sold;
And these, and all, are all amiss employed.
What would you have me do? I am a subject,
134 And I challenge law. Attorneys are denied me,
And therefore personally I lay my claim
136 To my inheritance of free descent.

NORTHUMBERLAND
The noble duke hath been too much abused.

ROSS
138 It stands your grace upon to do him right.

WILLOUGHBY
139 Base men by his endowments are made great.

YORK
My lords of England, let me tell you this:
I have had feeling of my cousin's wrongs,
And labored all I could to do him right;
143 But in this kind to come, in braving arms,
Be his own carver and cut out his way,

---

122 *unthrifts* spendthrifts   126 *first* i.e. before Gaunt   128 *rouse* rout from cover; *chase . . . bay* hunt them to the death   131 *distrained* seized   134 *challenge law* demand my rights   136 *my inheritance of* that which I inherit by   138 *It . . . upon* it's up to you   139 *his endowments* what they got from him   143 *kind* fashion

To find out right with wrong – it may not be ;
And you that do abet him in this kind
Cherish rebellion and are rebels all.

NORTHUMBERLAND
The noble duke hath sworn his coming is
But for his own ; and for the right of that
We all have strongly sworn to give him aid ;
And let him never see joy that breaks that oath !

YORK
Well, well, I see the issue of these arms.
I cannot mend it, I must needs confess,
Because my power is weak and all ill left ;   154
But if I could, by him that gave me life,
I would attach you all and make you stoop   156
Unto the sovereign mercy of the king ;
But since I cannot, be it known unto you
I do remain as neuter. So fare you well –   159
Unless you please to enter in the castle
And there repose you for this night.

BOLINGBROKE
An offer, uncle, that we will accept ;
But we must win your grace to go with us
To Bristol Castle, which they say is held
By Bushy, Bagot, and their complices,
The caterpillars of the commonwealth,   166
Which I have sworn to weed and pluck away.   167

YORK
It may be I will go with you ; but yet I'll pause,
For I am loath to break our country's laws.
Nor friends nor foes, to me welcome you are.   170
Things past redress are now with me past care.   *Exeunt.*

*

154 *all ill left* everything left in disorder   156 *attach* arrest   159 *neuter*
neutral   166 *caterpillars* i.e. devourers   167 *weed* get rid of   170 *Nor . . .
are* as a neutral I welcome you

75

II, iv   *Enter Earl of Salisbury and a Welsh Captain.*

WELSH CAPTAIN

My Lord of Salisbury, we have stayed ten days
2   And hardly kept our countrymen together,
And yet we hear no tidings from the king.
Therefore we will disperse ourselves. Farewell.

SALISBURY

Stay yet another day, thou trusty Welshman.
The king reposeth all his confidence in thee.

WELSH CAPTAIN

'Tis thought the king is dead. We will not stay.
8   The bay trees in our country all are withered,
And meteors fright the fixèd stars of heaven;
The pale-faced moon looks bloody on the earth,
11   And lean-looked prophets whisper fearful change;
Rich men look sad, and ruffians dance and leap –
The one in fear to lose what they enjoy,
14   The other to enjoy by rage and war.
These signs forerun the death or fall of kings.
Farewell. Our countrymen are gone and fled,
17   As well assured Richard their king is dead.   *[Exit.]*

SALISBURY

Ah, Richard! with the eyes of heavy mind,
I see thy glory, like a shooting star,
Fall to the base earth from the firmament.
Thy sun sets weeping in the lowly west,
22   Witnessing storms to come, woe, and unrest;
23   Thy friends are fled to wait upon thy foes,
24   And crossly to thy good all fortune goes.   *[Exit.]*

*

II, iv A Welsh camp s.d. *Welsh Captain* (perhaps the famous Owen
Glendower who is mentioned in III, i, 43 and appears in *1 Henry IV*) 2
hardly with difficulty 8–10 *The . . . earth* i.e. earth and the heavens show
omens of disaster 11 *change* political upheaval 14 *to enjoy* in hope to
enjoy; *rage* violence 17 *As* as being 22 *Witnessing* betokening 23 *wait
upon* offer allegiance to 24 *crossly* adversely

Enter [Bolingbroke] Duke of Hereford, York,   III, i
Northumberland, [Ross, Percy, Willoughby, with]
Bushy and Green prisoners.

BOLINGBROKE

Bring forth these men.
Bushy and Green, I will not vex your souls
(Since presently your souls must part your bodies)   3
With too much urging your pernicious lives,   4
For 'twere no charity; yet, to wash your blood
From off my hands, here in the view of men
I will unfold some causes of your deaths.
You have misled a prince, a royal king,
A happy gentleman in blood and lineaments,
By you unhappied and disfigured clean.   10
You have in manner with your sinful hours   11
Made a divorce betwixt his queen and him,
Broke the possession of a royal bed,
And stained the beauty of a fair queen's cheeks
With tears drawn from her eyes by your foul wrongs.
Myself – a prince by fortune of my birth,
Near to the king in blood, and near in love
Till you did make him misinterpret me –
Have stooped my neck under your injuries
And sighed my English breath in foreign clouds,   20
Eating the bitter bread of banishment,
Whilst you have fed upon my signories,   22
Disparked my parks and felled my forest woods,   23
From my own windows torn my household coat,   24
Rased out my imprese, leaving me no sign,   25
Save men's opinions and my living blood,
To show the world I am a gentleman.

III, i Before Bristol Castle   3 *part* leave   4 *urging* stressing   10 *clean* completely   11–12 *You have in manner . . . Made a divorce* you have . . . made a kind of divorce   20 *foreign clouds* clouds of breath exhaled in a foreign land   22 *signories* domains   23 *Disparked* thrown open to other uses   24 *torn* broken; *coat* coat of arms   25 *Rased out* erased; *imprese* heraldic emblem

This and much more, much more than twice all this,
Condemns you to the death. See them delivered over
To execution and the hand of death.

BUSHY

More welcome is the stroke of death to me
Than Bolingbroke to England. Lords, farewell.

GREEN

My comfort is that heaven will take our souls
And plague injustice with the pains of hell.

BOLINGBROKE

My Lord Northumberland, see them dispatched.
                    [*Exeunt Northumberland and others,*
                               with the prisoners.]

Uncle, you say the queen is at your house.
37   For God's sake, fairly let her be entreated.
38   Tell her I send to her my kind commends;
Take special care my greetings be delivered.

YORK

A gentleman of mine I have dispatched
41   With letters of your love to her at large.

BOLINGBROKE

Thanks, gentle uncle. Come, lords, away,
43   To fight with Glendower and his complices.
44   A while to work, and after holiday.   *Exeunt.*

*

III, ii   [*Drums. Flourish and Colors.*] *Enter the King,
                 Aumerle, [the Bishop of] Carlisle, &c. [Soldiers and
                 Attendants*].

KING

Barkloughly Castle call they this at hand?

AUMERLE

2   Yea, my lord. How brooks your grace the air

37 *entreated* treated   38 *commends* remembrances   41 *at large* conveyed in
full   43 *Glendower* (see II, iv, s.d.n.)   44 *after* afterwards
III, ii Before Barkloughly Castle (Harlech in Wales)   2 *brooks* enjoys

After your late tossing on the breaking seas?

KING
Needs must I like it well. I weep for joy
To stand upon my kingdom once again.
Dear earth, I do salute thee with my hand,
Though rebels wound thee with their horses' hoofs.
As a long-parted mother with her child   8
Plays fondly with her tears and smiles in meeting,   9
So weeping, smiling, greet I thee, my earth,
And do thee favors with my royal hands.   11
Feed not thy sovereign's foe, my gentle earth,
Nor with thy sweets comfort his ravenous sense;
But let thy spiders that suck up thy venom,
And heavy-gaited toads, lie in their way,
Doing annoyance to the treacherous feet
Which with usurping steps do trample thee.
Yield stinging nettles to mine enemies;
And when they from thy bosom pluck a flower,
Guard it, I pray thee, with a lurking adder
Whose double tongue may with a mortal touch   21
Throw death upon thy sovereign's enemies.
Mock not my senseless conjuration, lords.   23
This earth shall have a feeling, and these stones
Prove armèd soldiers ere her native king   25
Shall falter under foul rebellion's arms.

CARLISLE
Fear not, my lord. That Power that made you king
Hath power to keep you king in spite of all.
The means that heavens yield must be embraced
And not neglected. Else heaven would,
And we will not. Heaven's offer we refuse,
The proffered means of succor and redress.

---

8 *long-parted mother with* mother long parted from   9 *fondly* dotingly
11 *do . . . hands* salute thee by touching   21 *double* forked; *touch* wound
23 *senseless conjuration* solemn entreaty to things which cannot understand
it   25 *native* legitimate (Richard was born at Bordeaux)

AUMERLE

He means, my lord, that we are too remiss,

34   Whilst Bolingbroke, through our security,

Grows strong and great in substance and in power.

KING

36   Discomfortable cousin! know'st thou not

37   That when the searching eye of heaven is hid

Behind the globe, that lights the lower world,

Then thieves and robbers range abroad unseen

In murders and in outrage boldly here;

But when from under this terrestrial ball

He fires the proud tops of the eastern pines

And darts his light through every guilty hole,

Then murders, treasons, and detested sins,

The cloak of night being plucked from off their backs,

Stand bare and naked, trembling at themselves?

So when this thief, this traitor Bolingbroke,

Who all this while hath revelled in the night

49   Whilst we were wand'ring with the Antipodes,

Shall see us rising in our throne, the east,

His treasons will sit blushing in his face,

Not able to endure the sight of day,

But self-affrighted tremble at his sin.

Not all the water in the rough rude sea

55   Can wash the balm off from an anointed king.

56   The breath of worldly men cannot depose

The deputy elected by the Lord.

58   For every man that Bolingbroke hath pressed

59   To lift shrewd steel against our golden crown,

God for his Richard hath in heavenly pay

A glorious angel. Then, if angels fight,

Weak men must fall; for heaven still guards the right.

---

34 *security* overconfidence   **36** *Discomfortable* discouraging   **37–38** *when
. . . world* when the sun, lighting the other side of the world, is hidden from
view   **49** *Antipodes* the people on the other side of the world   **55** *balm*
consecrated oil used in the coronation   **56** *worldly* earthly   **58** *pressed*
drafted   **59** *shrewd* keen

Enter Salisbury.

Welcome, my lord. How far off lies your power ?   63

SALISBURY

Nor near nor farther off, my gracious lord,   64
Than this weak arm. Discomfort guides my tongue
And bids me speak of nothing but despair.
One day too late, I fear me, noble lord,
Hath clouded all thy happy days on earth.
O, call back yesterday, bid time return,
And thou shalt have twelve thousand fighting men !
To-day, to-day, unhappy day too late,
O'erthrows thy joys, friends, fortune, and thy state ;
For all the Welshmen, hearing thou wert dead,
Are gone to Bolingbroke, dispersed, and fled.

AUMERLE

Comfort, my liege. Why looks your grace so pale ?

KING

But now the blood of twenty thousand men   76
  Did triumph in my face, and they are fled ;
And, till so much blood thither come again,
  Have I not reason to look pale and dead ?
All souls that will be safe, fly from my side ;
For time hath set a blot upon my pride.

AUMERLE

Comfort, my liege. Remember who you are.

KING

I had forgot myself. Am I not king ?
Awake, thou coward majesty ! thou sleepest.
Is not the king's name twenty thousand names ?
Arm, arm, my name ! A puny subject strikes
At thy great glory. Look not to the ground,
Ye favorites of a king. Are we not high ?
High be our thoughts. I know my uncle York
Hath power enough to serve our turn. But who comes
  here ?

63 *power* army **64** *near* nearer **76** *twenty* (Richard exaggerates Salisbury's *twelve*)

Enter Scroop.

SCROOP

More health and happiness betide my liege
Than can my care-tuned tongue deliver him!

KING

Mine ear is open and my heart prepared.
94   The worst is worldly loss thou canst unfold.
Say, is my kingdom lost? Why, 'twas my care;
And what loss is it to be rid of care?
Strives Bolingbroke to be as great as we?
Greater he shall not be; if he serve God,
We'll serve him too, and be his fellow so.
Revolt our subjects? That we cannot mend;
They break their faith to God as well as us.
Cry woe, destruction, ruin, and decay:
The worst is death, and death will have his day.

SCROOP

Glad am I that your highness is so armed
To bear the tidings of calamity.
Like an unseasonable stormy day
Which makes the silver rivers drown their shores
As if the world were all dissolved to tears,
109   So high above his limits swells the rage
Of Bolingbroke, covering your fearful land
With hard bright steel, and hearts harder than steel.
112   White-beards have armed their thin and hairless scalps
Against thy majesty. Boys with women's voices
114   Strive to speak big, and clap their female joints
In stiff unwieldy arms against thy crown.
116   Thy very beadsmen learn to bend their bows
117   Of double-fatal yew against thy state.
118   Yea, distaff-women manage rusty bills

94 *The worst . . . unfold* the worst thou canst unfold is worldly loss 109
his limits its banks 112 *thin* sparsely haired 114 *clap* thrust; *female* i.e.
weak 116 *beadsmen* old pensioners who pray for their benefactor 117
double-fatal poisonous and used to make war-bows 118 *distaff-women*
spinning women; *manage* wield; *bills* halberds

Against thy seat. Both young and old rebel,   119
And all goes worse than I have power to tell.

KING

Too well, too well thou tell'st a tale so ill.
Where is the Earl of Wiltshire? Where is Bagot?
What is become of Bushy? Where is Green?
That they have let the dangerous enemy
Measure our confines with such peaceful steps?   125
If we prevail, their heads shall pay for it.
I warrant they have made peace with Bolingbroke.

SCROOP

Peace have they made with him indeed, my lord.

KING

O villains, vipers, damned without redemption!
Dogs easily won to fawn on any man!
Snakes in my heart-blood warmed that sting my heart!
Three Judases, each one thrice worse than Judas!
Would they make peace? Terrible hell make war
Upon their spotted souls for this offense!   134

SCROOP

Sweet love, I see, changing his property,   135
Turns to the sourest and most deadly hate.
Again uncurse their souls. Their peace is made
With heads, and not with hands. Those whom you curse 138
Have felt the worst of death's destroying wound
And lie full low, graved in the hollow ground.

AUMERLE

Is Bushy, Green, and the Earl of Wiltshire dead?

SCROOP

Ay, all of them at Bristol lost their heads.

AUMERLE

Where is the duke my father with his power?

KING

No matter where. Of comfort no man speak!

119 *seat* throne   125 *Measure* travel over   134 *spotted* stained with treason
135 *property* distinctive quality   138 *with hands* by lifting their hands in
surrender

Let's talk of graves, of worms, and epitaphs,
Make dust our paper, and with rainy eyes
Write sorrow on the bosom of the earth.
Let's choose executors and talk of wills.
And yet not so – for what can we bequeath,
Save our deposèd bodies to the ground ?
Our lands, our lives, and all are Bolingbroke's,
And nothing can we call our own but death
153   And that small model of the barren earth
Which serves as paste and cover to our bones.
For God's sake let us sit upon the ground
And tell sad stories of the death of kings !
How some have been deposed, some slain in war,
158   Some haunted by the ghosts they have deposed,
Some poisoned by their wives, some sleeping killed –
All murdered ; for within the hollow crown
That rounds the mortal temples of a king
162   Keeps Death his court ; and there the antic sits,
Scoffing his state and grinning at his pomp ;
164   Allowing him a breath, a little scene,
To monarchize, be feared, and kill with looks ;
166   Infusing him with self and vain conceit,
As if this flesh which walls about our life
168   Were brass impregnable ; and humored thus,
169   Comes at the last, and with a little pin
Bores through his castle wall, and farewell king !
Cover your heads, and mock not flesh and blood
With solemn reverence. Throw away respect,
Tradition, form, and ceremonious duty ;
For you have but mistook me all this while.

153–54 *that . . . bones* that mould of earth that covers our bones – the body
158 *the ghosts . . . deposed* the ghosts of the kings they have murdered   162
antic clown   164–65 *scene, To monarchize* time on life's stage to play the
monarch   166 *self . . . conceit* vain conceit of himself   168 *humored thus*
while the king is thus puffed up   169 *Comes* Death comes

I live with bread like you, feel want, taste grief,
Need friends. Subjected thus,   176
How can you say to me I am a king?

CARLISLE
My lord, wise men ne'er sit and wail their woes,
But presently prevent the ways to wail.   179
To fear the foe, since fear oppresseth strength,
Gives, in your weakness, strength unto your foe,
And so your follies fight against yourself.
Fear, and be slain – no worse can come to fight;   183
And fight and die is death destroying death,
Where fearing dying pays death servile breath.   185

AUMERLE
My father hath a power. Inquire of him,   186
And learn to make a body of a limb.

KING
Thou chid'st me well. Proud Bolingbroke, I come
To change blows with thee for our day of doom.
This ague fit of fear is overblown.
An easy task it is to win our own.
Say, Scroop, where lies our uncle with his power?
Speak sweetly, man, although thy looks be sour.

SCROOP
Men judge by the complexion of the sky
   The state and inclination of the day;   195
So may you by my dull and heavy eye:
   My tongue hath but a heavier tale to say.
I play the torturer, by small and small   198
To lengthen out the worst that must be spoken.
Your uncle York is joined with Bolingbroke,
And all your northern castles yielded up,

176 *Subjected thus* subject as I am – to these universal human needs   179
prevent . . . wail block the paths to grief   183 *to fight* by fighting   185 *Where*
whereas; *fearing dying* to be afraid to die   186 *of* about   195 *inclination . . .*
day trend of the weather   198–99 *by . . . spoken* in breaking the worst news
little by little

> And all your southern gentlemen in arms
> Upon his party.
>
> KING   Thou hast said enough.
>   *[To Aumerle]*
204 Beshrew thee, cousin, which didst lead me forth
> Of that sweet way I was in to despair!
> What say you now? What comfort have we now?
> By heaven, I'll hate him everlastingly
> That bids me be of comfort any more.
> Go to Flint Castle. There I'll pine away;
> A king, woe's slave, shall kingly woe obey.
> That power I have, discharge; and let them go
212 To ear the land that hath some hope to grow,
> For I have none. Let no man speak again
> To alter this, for counsel is but vain.
>
> AUMERLE
> My liege, one word.
>
> KING   He does me double wrong
> That wounds me with the flatteries of his tongue.
> Discharge my followers. Let them hence away,
> From Richard's night to Bolingbroke's fair day.
>   *[Exeunt.]*

*

III, iii   *Enter [with Drum and Colors] Bolingbroke, York,*
>   *Northumberland [, Attendants, and Soldiers].*
>
> BOLINGBROKE
1 So that by this intelligence we learn
> The Welshmen are dispersed, and Salisbury
> Is gone to meet the king, who lately landed
> With some few private friends upon this coast.
>
> NORTHUMBERLAND
5 The news is very fair and good, my lord,
> Richard not far from hence hath hid his head.

---

204 *Beshrew thee* confound you; *forth* out   **212** *ear* plough
III, iii Before Flint Castle in Wales   **1** *intelligence* news   **5–6** *The . . . head*
the news that Richard is in hiding not far away is auspicious and good

YORK
It would beseem the Lord Northumberland
To say 'King Richard.' Alack the heavy day
When such a sacred king should hide his head!

NORTHUMBERLAND
Your grace mistakes. Only to be brief,
Left I his title out.

YORK   The time hath been,
Would you have been so brief with him, he would
Have been so brief with you to shorten you,   13
For taking so the head, your whole head's length.   14

BOLINGBROKE
Mistake not, uncle, further than you should.

YORK
Take not, good cousin, further than you should,
Lest you mistake the heavens are over our heads.   17

BOLINGBROKE
I know it, uncle, and oppose not myself
Against their will. But who comes here?
    Enter Percy.
Welcome, Harry. What, will not this castle yield?

PERCY
The castle royally is manned, my lord,
Against thy entrance.

BOLINGBROKE
Royally?
Why, it contains no king?

PERCY   Yes, my good lord,
It doth contain a king. King Richard lies
Within the limits of yon lime and stone;
And with him are the Lord Aumerle, Lord Salisbury,
Sir Stephen Scroop, besides a clergyman
Of holy reverence – who, I cannot learn.

NORTHUMBERLAND
O, belike it is the Bishop of Carlisle.   30

13 *to* as to   14 *taking . . . head* thus omitting his title   17 *mistake* ignore the
fact that

87

BOLINGBROKE
Noble lords,
Go to the rude ribs of that ancient castle ;
Through brazen trumpet send the breath of parley
Into his ruined ears, and thus deliver :
Henry Bolingbroke
On both his knees doth kiss King Richard's hand
And sends allegiance and true faith of heart
To his most royal person ; hither come
Even at his feet to lay my arms and power,
40 Provided that my banishment repealed
And lands restored again be freely granted.
If not, I'll use the advantage of my power,
And lay the summer's dust with show'rs of blood
Rained from the wounds of slaughtered Englishmen ;
The which, how far off from the mind of Bolingbroke
It is, such crimson tempest should bedrench
The fresh green lap of fair King Richard's land,
48 My stooping duty tenderly shall show.
Go signify as much, while here we march
Upon the grassy carpet of this plain.
Let's march without the noise of threat'ning drum,
52 That from this castle's tottered battlements
53 Our fair appointments may be well perused.
Methinks King Richard and myself should meet
With no less terror than the elements
56 Of fire and water when their thund'ring shock
At meeting tears the cloudy cheeks of heaven.
Be he the fire, I'll be the yielding water ;
59 The rage be his, whilst on the earth I rain.
60 My water's on the earth, and not on him.
March on, and mark King Richard how he looks.

---

40 *repealed* revoked **48** *stooping duty* submissive kneeling; *tenderly*
considerately **52** *tottered* tattered, saw-toothed, crenellated **53** *appointments* equipment **56** *fire and water* lightning and clouds **59** *rain* 'reign'
60 *My . . . him* I fall upon the land, not upon him

*The trumpets sound [a parle without and within, then
a flourish. King] Richard appeareth on the walls
[with the Bishop of Carlisle, Aumerle, Scroop, and
Salisbury].*

See, see, King Richard doth himself appear,
As doth the blushing discontented sun
From out the fiery portal of the east
When he perceives the envious clouds are bent   65
To dim his glory and to stain the track
Of his bright passage to the occident.

YORK

Yet looks he like a king. Behold, his eye,   68
As bright as is the eagle's, lightens forth   69
Controlling majesty. Alack, alack, for woe,
That any harm should stain so fair a show!

KING *[to Northumberland]*

We are amazed; and thus long have we stood   72
To watch the fearful bending of thy knee,
Because we thought ourself thy lawful king.
And if we be, how dare thy joints forget
To pay their awful duty to our presence?   76
If we be not, show us the hand of God
That hath dismissed us from our stewardship;
For well we know no hand of blood and bone
Can gripe the sacred handle of our sceptre,
Unless he do profane, steal, or usurp.
And though you think that all, as you have done,
Have torn their souls by turning them from us   83
And we are barren and bereft of friends,
Yet know, my master, God omnipotent,
Is mustering in his clouds on our behalf
Armies of pestilence, and they shall strike
Your children yet unborn and unbegot   88
That lift your vassal hands against my head   89

65 *he* the sun 68 *he* King Richard 69 *lightens forth* flashes out 72
amazed in a maze, utterly confused 76 *awful duty* awed obeisance 83
torn torn asunder 88–89 *Your ... That* of you ... who 89 *vassal* subject

And threat the glory of my precious crown.
Tell Bolingbroke, for yon methinks he stands,
That every stride he makes upon my land
93   Is dangerous treason. He is come to open
The purple testament of bleeding war.
But ere the crown he looks for live in peace,
Ten thousand bloody crowns of mothers' sons
97   Shall ill become the flower of England's face,
Change the complexion of her maid-pale peace
To scarlet indignation, and bedew
100   Her pastor's grass with faithful English blood.

NORTHUMBERLAND
The King of Heaven forbid our lord the king
102   Should so with civil and uncivil arms
Be rushed upon! Thy thrice-noble cousin
Harry Bolingbroke doth humbly kiss thy hand;
And by the honorable tomb he swears
That stands upon your royal grandsire's bones,
And by the royalties of both your bloods
(Currents that spring from one most gracious head),
And by the buried hand of warlike Gaunt,
And by the worth and honor of himself,
Comprising all that may be sworn or said,
His coming hither hath no further scope
113   Than for his lineal royalties, and to beg
114   Enfranchisement immediate on his knees;
115   Which on thy royal party granted once,
116   His glittering arms he will commend to rust,
117   His barbèd steeds to stables, and his heart
To faithful service of your majesty.
This swears he, as he is a prince and just;

93–94 *open . . . war* carry out the terms of war's bloody will   97 *flower . . .
face* blooming surface of the land   100 *Her pastor's* her shepherd's, i.e.
Richard's   102 *civil* borne by Englishmen against Englishmen; *uncivil*
rude   113 *lineal royalties* royal birthrights   114 *Enfranchisement* freedom
from banishment   115 *on . . . party* on your majesty's part   116 *commend*
hand over   117 *barbèd* armored

And as I am a gentleman, I credit him.

KING

Northumberland, say thus. The king returns :   121
His noble cousin is right welcome hither ;
And all the number of his fair demands
Shall be accomplished without contradiction.
With all the gracious utterance thou hast
Speak to his gentle hearing kind commends.   126
          [To Aumerle]
We do debase ourselves, cousin, do we not,
To look so poorly and to speak so fair ?
Shall we call back Northumberland and send
Defiance to the traitor, and so die ?

AUMERLE

No, good my lord. Let's fight with gentle words
Till time lend friends, and friends their helpful swords.

KING

O God, O God ! that e'er this tongue of mine
That laid the sentence of dread banishment
On yon proud man, should take it off again
With words of sooth ! O that I were as great   136
As is my grief, or lesser than my name !   137
Or that I could forget what I have been !
Or not remember what I must be now !
Swell'st thou, proud heart ? I'll give thee scope to beat,   140
Since foes have scope to beat both thee and me.   141

AUMERLE

Northumberland comes back from Bolingbroke.

KING

What must the king do now ? Must he submit ?
The king shall do it. Must he be deposed ?
The king shall be contented. Must he lose
The name of king ? A God's name, let it go !   146
I'll give my jewels for a set of beads,   147

121 *returns* replies as follows   126 *commends* regards   136 *sooth* flattery
137 *name* title of king   140 *scope* room, permission   141 *have scope* aim
146 *A* in   147 *set of beads* rosary

My gorgeous palace for a hermitage,
149 My gay apparel for an almsman's gown,
150 My figured goblets for a dish of wood,
151 My sceptre for a palmer's walking staff,
My subjects for a pair of carvèd saints,
And my large kingdom for a little grave,
A little little grave, an obscure grave;
Or I'll be buried in the king's high way,
156 Some way of common trade, where subjects' feet
May hourly trample on their sovereign's head;
For on my heart they tread now whilst I live,
And buried once, why not upon my head?
Aumerle, thou weep'st, my tender-hearted cousin!
We'll make foul weather with despisèd tears;
162 Our sighs and they shall lodge the summer corn
163 And make a dearth in this revolting land.
164 Or shall we play the wantons with our woes
And make some pretty match with shedding tears?
As thus – to drop them still upon one place
167 Till they have fretted us a pair of graves
Within the earth; and therein laid – there lies
Two kinsmen digged their graves with weeping eyes.
Would not this ill do well? Well, well, I see
I talk but idly, and you laugh at me.
Most mighty prince, my Lord Northumberland,
What says King Bolingbroke? Will his majesty
Give Richard leave to live till Richard die?
175 You make a leg, and Bolingbroke says ay.

NORTHUMBERLAND
176 My lord, in the base court he doth attend
To speak with you, may it please you to come down.

---

149 *almsman* one living on charity   150 *figured* embossed   151 *palmer*
pilgrim   156 *trade* passage   162 *lodge* beat down   163 *revolting* rebelling
164 *play the wantons* sport   167 *fretted us* washed out for us   175 *You...ay*
if you curtsy to him, Bolingbroke will say yes   176 *base court* lower or outer
courtyard; *attend* wait

KING
>Down, down I come, like glist'ring Phaeton,   178
>Wanting the manage of unruly jades.   179
>In the base court? Base court, where kings grow base,
>To come at traitors' calls and do them grace!
>In the base court come down? Down court! down king!
>For night owls shriek where mounting larks should sing.
>>*[Exeunt from above.]*

BOLINGBROKE
>What says his majesty?

NORTHUMBERLAND   Sorrow and grief of heart
>Makes him speak fondly, like a frantic man.   185
>Yet he is come.
>>*[Enter King Richard attended, below.]*

BOLINGBROKE
>Stand all apart
>And show fair duty to his majesty.
>>*He kneels down.*
>My gracious lord –

KING
>Fair cousin, you debase your princely knee
>To make the base earth proud with kissing it.
>Me rather had my heart might feel your love   192
>Than my unpleased eye see your courtesy.
>Up, cousin, up! Your heart is up, I know,
>Thus high at least *[touches his own head]*, although your
>   knee be low.

BOLINGBROKE *[rises]*
>My gracious lord, I come but for mine own.

KING
>Your own is yours, and I am yours, and all.

BOLINGBROKE
>So far be mine, my most redoubted lord,   198

178 *Phaeton* (he borrowed the chariot of his father, the sun god, drove it unskillfully, nearly set the world on fire)   **179** *Wanting . . . of* lacking control over; *jades* poor horses   **185** *fondly* foolishly; *frantic* mad   **192** *Me rather had* I would rather   **198** *redoubted* dread

As my true service shall deserve your love.

KING
Well you deserve. They well deserve to have
That know the strong'st and surest way to get.
Uncle, give me your hand. Nay, dry your eyes.
203   Tears show their love, but want their remedies.
Cousin, I am too young to be your father,
Though you are old enough to be my heir.
What you will have, I'll give, and willing too ;
For do we must what force will have us do.
Set on towards London. Cousin, is it so ?

BOLINGBROKE
Yea, my good lord.

KING   Then I must not say no. *[Flourish. Exeunt.]*

*

III, iv   *Enter the Queen with [two Ladies,] her Attendants.*

QUEEN
What sport shall we devise here in this garden
To drive away the heavy thought of care ?

LADY
Madam, we'll play at bowls.

QUEEN
4   'Twill make me think the world is full of rubs
5   And that my fortune runs against the bias.

LADY
Madam, we'll dance.

QUEEN
7   My legs can keep no measure in delight
When my poor heart no measure keeps in grief.
Therefore no dancing, girl ; some other sport.

---

203 *want their remedies* cannot cure what causes them
III, iv The garden of the Duke of York's seat at Langley   4 *rubs* impedi-
ments (in the game of bowls)   5 *bias* curving course (of a bowl)   7–8
measure . . . measure stately dance . . . moderation

LADY
Madam, we'll tell tales.

QUEEN
Of sorrow or of joy?

LADY   Of either, madam.

QUEEN
Of neither, girl;
For if of joy, being altogether wanting,
It doth remember me the more of sorrow;
Or if of grief, being altogether had,   15
It adds more sorrow to my want of joy;
For what I have I need not to repeat,
And what I want it boots not to complain.   18

LADY
Madam, I'll sing.

QUEEN   'Tis well that thou hast cause;
But thou shouldst please me better, wouldst thou weep.

LADY
I could weep, madam, would it do you good.

QUEEN
And I could sing, would weeping do me good,
And never borrow any tear of thee.
        Enter Gardeners [one the Master, the other two his
        Men].
But stay, here come the gardeners.
Let's step into the shadow of these trees.
My wretchedness unto a row of pins,   26
They will talk of state, for every one doth so   27
Against a change: woe is forerun with woe.   28
        [Queen and Ladies step aside.]

GARDENER
Go bind thou up yon dangling apricocks,   29
Which, like unruly children, make their sire

---

15 *had* had by me   18 *boots* helps   26 *My . . . pins* my grief against a trifle
27 *state* politics   28 *Against* expecting   29 *apricocks* apricots

31 Stoop with oppression of their prodigal weight.
 Give some supportance to the bending twigs.
 Go thou and, like an executioner,
 Cut off the heads of too-fast-growing sprays
 That look too lofty in our commonwealth.
36 All must be even in our government.
 You thus employed, I will go root away
 The noisome weeds which without profit suck
 The soil's fertility from wholesome flowers.

[1.] MAN

40 Why should we, in the compass of a pale,
 Keep law and form and due proportion,
 Showing, as in a model, our firm estate,
 When our sea-wallèd garden, the whole land,
 Is full of weeds, her fairest flowers choked up,
 Her fruit trees all unpruned, her hedges ruined,
46 Her knots disordered, and her wholesome herbs
 Swarming with caterpillars?

GARDENER   Hold thy peace.
 He that hath suffered this disordered spring
 Hath now himself met with the fall of leaf.
 The weeds which his broad-spreading leaves did
  shelter,
51 That seemed in eating him to hold him up,
 Are plucked up root and all by Bolingbroke –
 I mean the Earl of Wiltshire, Bushy, Green.

[2.] MAN
 What, are they dead?

GARDENER   They are; and Bolingbroke
 Hath seized the wasteful king. O, what pity is it
 That he had not so trimmed and dressed his land
57 As we this garden! We at time of year

---

31 *prodigal* excessive 36 *even* equal 40 *pale* enclosed garden 46 *knots*
flower-beds laid out in patterns 51 *in* while 57 *at ... year* in season

Do wound the bark, the skin of our fruit trees,
Lest, being overproud in sap and blood,   59
With too much riches it confound itself.   60
Had he done so to great and growing men,
They might have lived to bear, and he to taste
Their fruits of duty. Superfluous branches
We lop away, that bearing boughs may live.
Had he done so, himself had borne the crown,
Which waste of idle hours hath quite thrown down.

[2.] MAN
What, think you the king shall be deposed?

GARDENER
Depressed he is already, and deposed   68
'Tis doubt he will be. Letters came last night   69
To a dear friend of the good Duke of York's
That tell black tidings.

QUEEN
O, I am pressed to death through want of speaking!   72
    [Comes forward.]
Thou old Adam's likeness, set to dress this garden,   73
How dares thy harsh rude tongue sound this unpleasing
    news?
What Eve, what serpent, hath suggested thee   75
To make a second fall of cursèd man?
Why dost thou say King Richard is deposed?
Dar'st thou, thou little better thing than earth,
Divine his downfall? Say, where, when, and how   79
Cam'st thou by this ill tidings? Speak, thou wretch!

GARDENER
Pardon me, madam. Little joy have I
To breathe this news; yet what I say is true.   82

59 *overproud in* swollen with   60 *confound* destroy   68 *Depressed* brought
low   69 *'Tis doubt* there is fear   72 *pressed to death* tortured as by a heavy
weight crushing me   73 *old Adam* the first gardener   75 *suggested* tempted
79 *Divine* prophesy by occult means   82 *To breathe* in speaking

King Richard, he is in the mighty hold
Of Bolingbroke. Their fortunes both are weighed.
In your lord's scale is nothing but himself,
And some few vanities that make him light;
But in the balance of great Bolingbroke,
Besides himself, are all the English peers,
And with that odds he weighs King Richard down.
Post you to London, and you will find it so.
I speak no more than every one doth know.

QUEEN

Nimble mischance, that art so light of foot,
93   Doth not thy embassage belong to me,
And am I last that knows it? O, thou thinkest
To serve me last, that I may longest keep
96   Thy sorrow in my breast. Come, ladies, go
To meet at London London's king in woe.
What, was I born to this, that my sad look
99   Should grace the triumph of great Bolingbroke?
Gard'ner, for telling me these news of woe,
Pray God the plants thou graft'st may never grow.

Exit [with Ladies].

GARDNER

Poor queen, so that thy state might be no worse,
I would my skill were subject to thy curse!
104   Here did she fall a tear; here in this place
105   I'll set a bank of rue, sour herb of grace.
106   Rue, even for ruth, here shortly shall be seen,
In the remembrance of a weeping queen.   *Exeunt.*

*

93 *embassage* message   96 *Thy sorrow* the sorrow you report   99 *triumph* triumphal procession; *Bolingbroke* (in the original spelling, 'Bulling-brooke,' the name rimes with *look* in l. 98)   104 *fall* drop   105 *grace* repentance   106 *ruth* pity

*Enter Bolingbroke, with the Lords [Aumerle,
Northumberland, Percy, Fitzwater, Surrey, and
another, with Bishop of Carlisle, Abbot of
Westminster, Attendants, and Herald] to
Parliament.*

BOLINGBROKE

Call forth Bagot.

Enter [Officers with] Bagot.

Now, Bagot, freely speak thy mind,
What thou dost know of noble Gloucester's death ;
Who wrought it with the king, and who performed   4
The bloody office of his timeless end.   5

BAGOT

Then set before my face the Lord Aumerle.

BOLINGBROKE

Cousin, stand forth, and look upon that man.

BAGOT

My Lord Aumerle, I know your daring tongue
Scorns to unsay what once it hath delivered.
In that dead time when Gloucester's death was plotted,   10
I heard you say, 'Is not my arm of length,   11
That reacheth from the restful English court   12
As far as Calais to mine uncle's head ?'
Amongst much other talk that very time
I heard you say that you had rather refuse
The offer of an hundred thousand crowns
Than Bolingbroke's return to England ;   17
Adding withal, how blest this land would be   18
In this your cousin's death.

AUMERLE   Princes and noble lords,
What answer shall I make to this base man ?
Shall I so much dishonor my fair stars   21

IV, i Westminster Hall (September–October, 1399) 4 *wrought . . . king*
worked on the king's mind to bring it about 5 *timeless* untimely 10 *dead*
dark, silent 11 *of length* long 12 *restful* calm, untroubled by Gloucester
17 *Than . . . return* than have Bolingbroke return 18 *withal* besides 21
fair stars high rank and fortune

22 On equal terms to give him chastisement?
     Either I must, or have mine honor soiled
24 With the attainder of his slanderous lips.
25 There is my gage, the manual seal of death
     That marks thee out for hell. I say thou liest,
     And will maintain what thou hast said is false
28 In thy heart-blood, though being all too base
29 To stain the temper of my knightly sword.

BOLINGBROKE
     Bagot, forbear; thou shalt not take it up.

AUMERLE
31 Excepting one, I would he were the best
32 In all this presence that hath moved me so.

FITZWATER
33 If that thy valor stand on sympathy,
     There is my gage, Aumerle, in gage to thine.
     By that fair sun which shows me where thou stand'st,
     I heard thee say, and vauntingly thou spak'st it,
     That thou wert cause of noble Gloucester's death.
     If thou deniest it twenty times, thou liest,
     And I will turn thy falsehood to thy heart,
     Where it was forgèd, with my rapier's point.

AUMERLE
     Thou dar'st not, coward, live to see that day.

FITZWATER
     Now, by my soul, I would it were this hour.

AUMERLE
     Fitzwater, thou art damned to hell for this.

PERCY
     Aumerle, thou liest. His honor is as true
45 In this appeal as thou art all unjust;
     And that thou art so, there I throw my gage

---

22 *On . . . chastisement* as to fight him as my equal in rank   **24** *attainder* disgraceful accusation   **25** *manual . . . death* your death warrant sealed by my hand   **28** *being* it is   **29** *temper* honorable quality   **31** *one* i.e. Bolingbroke   **32** *moved* angered   **33** *If . . . sympathy* if your valor can show itself only on those who are your equals in blood   **45** *all unjust* completely false

To prove it on thee to the extremest point
Of mortal breathing. Seize it if thou dar'st.

AUMERLE

And if I do not, may my hands rot off
And never brandish more revengeful steel
Over the glittering helmet of my foe !

ANOTHER LORD

I task the earth to the like, forsworn Aumerle ;   52
And spur thee on with full as many lies   53
As may be holloed in thy treacherous ear
From sun to sun. There is my honor's pawn.   55
Engage it to the trial, if thou darest.   56

AUMERLE

Who sets me else ? By heaven, I'll throw at all !   57
I have a thousand spirits in one breast
To answer twenty thousand such as you.

SURREY

My Lord Fitzwater, I do remember well
The very time Aumerle and you did talk.

FITZWATER

'Tis very true. You were in presence then,   62
And you can witness with me this is true.

SURREY

As false, by heaven, as heaven itself is true !

FITZWATER

Surrey, thou liest.

SURREY   Dishonorable boy !
That lie shall lie so heavy on my sword
That it shall render vengeance and revenge
Till thou the lie-giver and that lie do lie
In earth as quiet as thy father's skull.
In proof whereof there is my honor's pawn.
Engage it to the trial if thou dar'st.

---

52 *task . . . like* burden the ground with another gage   53 *lies* accusations of
lying   55 *pawn* pledge   56 *Engage . . . trial* take it as a challenge to fight   57
sets me puts up stakes against me; *throw at all* throw down gloves, like
wagers at dice, against you all   62 *in presence* present at court

FITZWATER

72   How fondly dost thou spur a forward horse!
      If I dare eat, or drink, or breathe, or live,

74   I dare meet Surrey in a wilderness,
      And spit upon him whilst I say he lies,
      And lies, and lies. There is my bond of faith
      To tie thee to my strong correction.

78   As I intend to thrive in this new world,
      Aumerle is guilty of my true appeal.
      Besides, I heard the banished Norfolk say
      That thou, Aumerle, didst send two of thy men
      To execute the noble duke at Calais.

AUMERLE

      Some honest Christian trust me with a gage
      That Norfolk lies. Here do I throw down this,

85   If he may be repealed to try his honor.

BOLINGBROKE

86   These differences shall all rest under gage
      Till Norfolk be repealed. Repealed he shall be
      And, though mine enemy, restored again
      To all his lands and signories. When he is returned,
      Against Aumerle we will enforce his trial.

CARLISLE

      That honorable day shall never be seen.
      Many a time hath banished Norfolk fought
      For Jesu Christ in glorious Christian field,

94   Streaming the ensign of the Christian cross
      Against black pagans, Turks, and Saracens;

96   And, toiled with works of war, retired himself
      To Italy; and there, at Venice, gave
      His body to that pleasant country's earth
      And his pure soul unto his captain, Christ,
      Under whose colors he had fought so long.

---

72 *forward* willing   **74** *in a wilderness* i.e. where there would be no help and
no escape   **78** *in . . . world* under the new king   **85** *repealed* called back   **86**
under gage as challenges   **94** *Streaming* flying   **96** *toiled* worn out

BOLINGBROKE
Why, Bishop, is Norfolk dead?

CARLISLE
As surely as I live, my lord.

BOLINGBROKE
Sweet peace conduct his sweet soul to the bosom   103
Of good old Abraham! Lords appellants,
Your differences shall all rest under gage
Till we assign you to your days of trial.
        Enter York [attended].

YORK
Great Duke of Lancaster, I come to thee
From plume-plucked Richard, who with willing soul   108
Adopts thee heir and his high sceptre yields
To the possession of thy royal hand.
Ascend his throne, descending now from him,
And long live Henry, fourth of that name!

BOLINGBROKE
In God's name I'll ascend the regal throne.

CARLISLE
Marry, God forbid!   114
Worst in this royal presence may I speak,   115
Yet, best beseeming me to speak the truth: 116
Would God that any in this noble presence
Were enough noble to be upright judge
Of noble Richard! then true noblesse would
Learn him forbearance from so foul a wrong.
What subject can give sentence on his king?
And who sits here that is not Richard's subject?
Thieves are not judged but they are by to hear,
Although apparent guilt be seen in them;
And shall the figure of God's majesty,
His captain, steward, deputy elect,

103-04 *bosom . . . Abraham* heavenly rest   108 *plume-plucked* sorry-looking,
denuded   114 *Marry* by the Virgin Mary   115 *Worst . . . speak* I may be by
birth and position the most unfit to speak   116 *best . . . truth* since it best
beseems me, a clergyman, to speak the truth, I say

Anointed, crownèd, planted many years,
Be judged by subject and inferior breath,
129 And he himself not present? O, forfend it God
130 That, in a Christian climate, souls refined
131 Should show so heinous, black, obscene a deed!
I speak to subjects, and a subject speaks,
Stirred up by God, thus boldly for his king.
My Lord of Hereford here, whom you call king,
Is a foul traitor to proud Hereford's king;
And if you crown him, let me prophesy,
The blood of English shall manure the ground
And future ages groan for this foul act;
Peace shall go sleep with Turks and infidels,
And in this seat of peace tumultuous wars
141 Shall kin with kin and kind with kind confound;
Disorder, horror, fear, and mutiny
Shall here inhabit, and this land be called
144 The field of Golgotha and dead men's skulls.
O, if you raise this house against this house,
It will the woefullest division prove
That ever fell upon this cursèd earth.
Prevent it, resist it, let it not be so,
Lest child, child's children cry against you woe.

NORTHUMBERLAND
Well have you argued, sir; and for your pains
151 Of capital treason we arrest you here.
My Lord of Westminster, be it your charge
To keep him safely till his day of trial.
154 [May it please you, lords, to grant the commons' suit.

BOLINGBROKE
Fetch hither Richard, that in common view
He may surrender. So we shall proceed

---

129 *forfend* forbid **130** *souls refined* civilized people **131** *obscene* ill-omened **141** *kin . . . kind* kinsmen . . . fellow-countrymen **144** *Golgotha* 'the place of a skull,' Calvary **151** *Of* on the charge of; *capital* carrying the death penalty **154–318** *May . . . fall* (see 'Note on the Text,' p. 22) **154** *suit* request that the causes of Richard's deposition be published

Without suspicion.
YORK   I will be his conduct.   *Exit.* 157
BOLINGBROKE
 Lords, you that here are under our arrest,
 Procure your sureties for your days of answer.   159
 Little are we beholding to your love,
 And little looked for at your helping hands.
  Enter Richard and York [with Officers bearing the
  crown, & c.].

RICHARD
 Alack, why am I sent for to a king
 Before I have shook off the regal thoughts
 Wherewith I reigned ? I hardly yet have learned
 To insinuate, flatter, bow, and bend my limbs.
 Give sorrow leave a while to tutor me
 To this submission. Yet I well remember
 The favors of these men. Were they not mine ?   168
 Did they not sometime cry 'All hail !' to me ?
 So Judas did to Christ ; but he, in twelve,
 Found truth in all but one ; I, in twelve thousand none.
 God save the king ! Will no man say amen ?
 Am I both priest and clerk ? Well then, amen !   173
 God save the king ! although I be not he ;
 And yet amen, if heaven do think him me.
 To do what service am I sent for hither ?

YORK
 To do that office of thine own good will
 Which tired majesty did make thee offer –   178
 The resignation of thy state and crown
 To Henry Bolingbroke.

RICHARD
 Give me the crown. Here, cousin, seize the crown.
 Here, cousin,

---

157 *conduct* escort   159 *sureties* men who will be responsible for your
appearance   168 *favors* faces and friendly acts   173 *Am . . . clerk* must I
pray like the priest and say amen like the clerk   178 *tired majesty* weariness
of kingship

On this side my hand, and on that side yours.
Now is this golden crown like a deep well
185 That owes two buckets, filling one another,
The emptier ever dancing in the air,
The other down, unseen, and full of water.
That bucket down and full of tears am I,
Drinking my griefs whilst you mount up on high.

BOLINGBROKE
I thought you had been willing to resign.

RICHARD
My crown I am, but still my griefs are mine.
You may my glories and my state depose,
But not my griefs. Still am I king of those.

BOLINGBROKE
Part of your cares you give me with your crown.

RICHARD
Your cares set up do not pluck my cares down.
196 My care is loss of care, by old care done;
197 Your care is gain of care, by new care won.
The cares I give I have, though given away;
199 They tend the crown, yet still with me they stay.

BOLINGBROKE
Are you contented to resign the crown?

RICHARD
201 Ay, no; no, ay; for I must nothing be;
Therefore no no, for I resign to thee.
203 Now mark me how I will undo myself.
I give this heavy weight from off my head
And this unwieldy sceptre from my hand,
The pride of kingly sway from out my heart.
With mine own tears I wash away my balm,
With mine own hands I give away my crown,
With mine own tongue deny my sacred state,

---

185 *owes* owns, has   196 *care . . . care . . . old care* grief . . . responsibility . . . failing diligence   197 *care . . . care . . . new care* anxiety . . . responsibility . . . fresh zeal   199 *tend* go with   201 *Ay . . . ay* 'yes, no; no, yes,' but also 'I, no; no I'   203 *undo* strip and ruin

With mine own breath release all duty's rites.   210
All pomp and majesty I do forswear ;
My manors, rents, revenues I forgo ;
My acts, decrees, and statutes I deny.
God pardon all oaths that are broke to me !
God keep all vows unbroke that swear to thee !   215
Make me, that nothing have, with nothing grieved,
And thou with all pleased, that hast all achieved !
Long mayst thou live in Richard's seat to sit,
And soon lie Richard in an earthy pit !
God save King Harry, unkinged Richard says,
And send him many years of sunshine days !
What more remains ?

NORTHUMBERLAND No more, but that you read
These accusations and these grievous crimes
Committed by your person and your followers
Against the state and profit of this land,   225
That, by confessing them, the souls of men
May deem that you are worthily deposed.   227

RICHARD
Must I do so ? and must I ravel out   228
My weaved-up folly ? Gentle Northumberland,
If thy offenses were upon record,
Would it not shame thee in so fair a troop
To read a lecture of them ? If thou wouldst,   232
There shouldst thou find one heinous article,
Containing the deposing of a king
And cracking the strong warrant of an oath,   235
Marked with a blot, damned in the book of heaven.
Nay, all of you that stand and look upon
Whilst that my wretchedness doth bait myself,   238
Though some of you, with Pilate, wash your hands,
Showing an outward pity, yet you Pilates

---

210 *duty's rites* ceremonies of respect 215 *swear* are sworn 225 *state and profit* ordered prosperity 227 *worthily* justly 228 *ravel out* unravel 232 *read . . . them* read them out like the lesson in church 235 *oath* i.e. your oath of allegiance to me 238 *bait* torment

241   Have here delivered me to my sour cross,
And water cannot wash away your sin.

NORTHUMBERLAND

243   My lord, dispatch. Read o'er these articles.

RICHARD

Mine eyes are full of tears; I cannot see.
And yet salt water blinds them not so much
246   But they can see a sort of traitors here.
Nay, if I turn mine eyes upon myself,
I find myself a traitor with the rest;
For I have given here my soul's consent
250   To undeck the pompous body of a king;
Made glory base, and sovereignty a slave,
Proud majesty a subject, state a peasant.

NORTHUMBERLAND

My lord –

RICHARD

254   No lord of thine, thou haught, insulting man,
Nor no man's lord. I have no name, no title –
256   No, not that name was given me at the font –
But 'tis usurped. Alack the heavy day,
That I have worn so many winters out
And know not now what name to call myself!
O that I were a mockery king of snow,
Standing before the sun of Bolingbroke
To melt myself away in water drops!
Good king, great king, and yet not greatly good,
264   An if my word be sterling yet in England,
Let it command a mirror hither straight,
That it may show me what a face I have
Since it is bankrout of his majesty.

BOLINGBROKE

Go some of you and fetch a looking glass.
[Exit an Attendant.]

241 *sour* bitter 243 *dispatch* make haste 246 *sort* gang 250 *pompous* stately
254 *haught* arrogant 256–57 *No . . . usurped* (Richard's enemies spread
a rumor that he was illegitimate) 264 *An if* if; *sterling* valid currency

NORTHUMBERLAND
Read o'er this paper while the glass doth come.

RICHARD
Fiend, thou torments me ere I come to hell!   270

BOLINGBROKE
Urge it no more, my Lord Northumberland.

NORTHUMBERLAND
The commons will not then be satisfied.

RICHARD
They shall be satisfied. I'll read enough
When I do see the very book indeed
Where all my sins are writ, and that's myself.
      Enter one with a glass.
Give me the glass, and therein will I read.
No deeper wrinkles yet? Hath sorrow struck
So many blows upon this face of mine
And made no deeper wounds? O flattering glass,
Like to my followers in prosperity,
Thou dost beguile me! Was this face the face
That every day under his household roof
Did keep ten thousand men? Was this the face
That like the sun did make beholders wink?   284
Was this the face that faced so many follies   285
And was at last outfaced by Bolingbroke?
A brittle glory shineth in this face.
As brittle as the glory is the face,
      [Dashes the glass to the floor.]
For there it is, cracked in a hundred shivers.
Mark, silent king, the moral of this sport —
How soon my sorrow hath destroyed my face.

BOLINGBROKE
The shadow of your sorrow hath destroyed   292
The shadow of your face.

RICHARD   Say that again.
The shadow of my sorrow? Ha! let's see!

284 *wink* close their eyes   285 *faced* countenanced   292–93 *shadow* . . .
shadow outward show . . . reflection

'Tis very true : my grief lies all within ;
And these external manners of laments
Are merely shadows to the unseen grief
That swells with silence in the tortured soul.
There lies the substance ; and I thank thee, king,
300 For thy great bounty that not only giv'st
Me cause to wail, but teachest me the way
302 How to lament the cause. I'll beg one boon,
And then be gone and trouble you no more.
Shall I obtain it ?

BOLINGBROKE   Name it, fair cousin.

RICHARD
Fair cousin ? I am greater than a king ;
For when I was a king, my flatterers
Were then but subjects ; being now a subject,
308 I have a king here to my flatterer.
Being so great, I have no need to beg.

BOLINGBROKE
Yet ask.

RICHARD
And shall I have ?

BOLINGBROKE
You shall.

RICHARD
Then give me leave to go.

BOLINGBROKE
Whither ?

RICHARD
Whither you will, so I were from your sights.

BOLINGBROKE
316 Go some of you, convey him to the Tower.

RICHARD
317 O, good ! Convey ? Conveyers are you all,
That rise thus nimbly by a true king's fall.]

[Exit Richard, with some Lords and a Guard.]

---

300 *that* who   **302** *boon* favor   **308** *to* as   **316** *convey* escort   **317** *Convey*
slang for 'steal'

BOLINGBROKE

On Wednesday next we solemnly proclaim
Our coronation. Lords, be ready all.
> *Exeunt. Manent [the Abbot of] Westminster,*
> *[the Bishop of] Carlisle, Aumerle.*

ABBOT

A woeful pageant have we here beheld.

CARLISLE

The woe's to come. The children yet unborn
Shall feel this day as sharp to them as thorn.

AUMERLE

You holy clergymen, is there no plot
To rid the realm of this pernicious blot?

ABBOT

My lord,
Before I freely speak my mind herein,
You shall not only take the sacrament
To bury mine intents, but also to effect   329
Whatever I shall happen to devise.
I see your brows are full of discontent,
Your hearts of sorrow, and your eyes of tears.
Come home with me to supper. I will lay
A plot shall show us all a merry day.   *Exeunt.*

*

Enter the Queen with [Ladies,] her Attendants.   V, i

QUEEN

This way the king will come. This is the way
To Julius Caesar's ill-erected tower,   2
To whose flint bosom my condemnèd lord
Is doomed a prisoner by proud Bolingbroke.
Here let us rest, if this rebellious earth
Have any resting for her true king's queen.

---

329 *bury mine intents* hide what I intend
V, i A London street   2 *ill-erected* erected with evil results

Enter Richard [and Guard].

But soft, but see, or rather do not see,
My fair rose wither. Yet look up, behold,
That you in pity may dissolve to dew
And wash him fresh again with true-love tears.

11   Ah, thou the model where old Troy did stand,
12   Thou map of honor, thou King Richard's tomb,
13   And not King Richard! Thou most beauteous inn,
Why should hard-favored grief be lodged in thee
When triumph is become an alehouse guest?

RICHARD
Join not with grief, fair woman, do not so,
To make my end too sudden. Learn, good soul,
To think our former state a happy dream;
From which awaked, the truth of what we are
Shows us but this. I am sworn brother, sweet,
To grim Necessity, and he and I
Will keep a league till death. Hie thee to France
And cloister thee in some religious house.

24   Our holy lives must win a new world's crown,
25   Which our profane hours here have thrown down.

QUEEN
What, is my Richard both in shape and mind
Transformed and weak'ned? Hath Bolingbroke deposed
Thine intellect? Hath he been in thy heart?
The lion dying thrusteth forth his paw
And wounds the earth, if nothing else, with rage

31   To be o'erpow'red; and wilt thou pupil-like
Take the correction mildly, kiss the rod,
And fawn on rage with base humility,
Which art a lion and the king of beasts?

RICHARD
A king of beasts indeed! If aught but beasts,

---

11 *model . . . stand* ground plan of ruin, like that of Troy after its fall   12 *map*
pattern   13–15 *inn . . . alehouse* mansion (Richard) . . . tavern (Bolingbroke)
24 *new world's* heavenly   25 *thrown* (two syllables)   31 *To be* at being

I had been still a happy king of men.
Good sometimes queen, prepare thee hence for France.
Think I am dead, and that even here thou takest,
As from my deathbed, thy last living leave.
In winter's tedious nights sit by the fire
With good old folks, and let them tell thee tales   41
Of woeful ages long ago betid;
And ere thou bid good night, to quite their griefs   43
Tell thou the lamentable tale of me,
And send the hearers weeping to their beds.
For why, the senseless brands will sympathize   46
The heavy accent of thy moving tongue
And in compassion weep the fire out;
And some will mourn in ashes, some coal-black,
For the deposing of a rightful king.
    Enter Northumberland [attended].

NORTHUMBERLAND
My lord, the mind of Bolingbroke is changed.
You must to Pomfret, not unto the Tower.   52
And, madam, there is order ta'en for you:
With all swift speed you must away to France.

RICHARD
Northumberland, thou ladder wherewithal   55
The mounting Bolingbroke ascends my throne,
The time shall not be many hours of age
More than it is, ere foul sin gathering head   58
Shall break into corruption. Thou shalt think,
Though he divide the realm and give thee half,
It is too little, helping him to all.
And he shall think that thou, which knowest the way
To plant unrightful kings, wilt know again,
Being ne'er so little urged another way,

41–42 *tales . . . betid* tales of woe which happened in ages long past   43
quite requite; *griefs* tales of woe   46 *For why* because; *sympathize* respond
to   52 *Pomfret* Pontefract, or Pomfret, Castle in Yorkshire (the scene of
V, v)   55 *wherewithal* by means of which   58 *gathering head* coming to a
head, like a boil

65   To pluck him headlong from the usurped throne.
66   The love of wicked men converts to fear ;
      That fear to hate, and hate turns one or both
68   To worthy danger and deservèd death.

NORTHUMBERLAND
      My guilt be on my head, and there an end !
70   Take leave and part, for you must part forthwith.

RICHARD
      Doubly divorced ! Bad men, you violate
      A twofold marriage – 'twixt my crown and me,
      And then betwixt me and my married wife.
      Let me unkiss the oath 'twixt thee and me ;
      And yet not so, for with a kiss 'twas made.
      Part us, Northumberland – I towards the north,
77   Where shivering cold and sickness pines the clime ;
      My wife to France, from whence, set forth in pomp,
      She came adornèd hither like sweet May,
80   Sent back like Hallowmas or short'st of day.

QUEEN
      And must we be divided ? Must we part ?

RICHARD
      Ay, hand from hand, my love, and heart from heart.

QUEEN
      Banish us both, and send the king with me.

NORTHUMBERLAND
84   That were some love, but little policy.

QUEEN
      Then whither he goes, thither let me go.

RICHARD
86   So two, together weeping, make one woe.
      Weep thou for me in France, I for thee here.
88   Better far off than near, be ne'er the near.

---

65 *To* how to   66 *converts* changes   68 *worthy* merited   70 *part . . . part* separate . . . depart   77 *pines the clime* make the climate an enfeebling one   80 *Hallowmas* All Saint's Day, November 1 ; *short'st of day* the winter solstice   84 *policy* political wisdom   86 *So* no, for thus   88 *near . . . near* being near, never be nearer

Go, count thy way with sighs; I mine with groans.

QUEEN

So longest way shall have the longest moans.

RICHARD

Twice for one step I'll groan, the way being short,
And piece the way out with a heavy heart.
Come, come, in wooing sorrow let's be brief,
Since, wedding it, there is such length in grief.
One kiss shall stop our mouths, and dumbly part.
Thus give I mine, and thus take I thy heart.

QUEEN

Give me mine own again. 'Twere no good part
To take on me to keep and kill thy heart.
So, now I have mine own again, be gone,
That I may strive to kill it with a groan.

RICHARD

We make woe wanton with this fond delay.   101
Once more adieu! The rest let sorrow say.   *Exeunt.*

*

Enter Duke of York and the Duchess.   V, ii

DUCHESS

My lord, you told me you would tell the rest,
When weeping made you break the story off
Of our two cousins coming into London.

YORK

Where did I leave?   4

DUCHESS   At that sad stop, my lord,
Where rude misgoverned hands from windows' tops   5
Threw dust and rubbish on King Richard's head.

YORK

Then, as I said, the duke, great Bolingbroke,
Mounted upon a hot and fiery steed

101 *We ... wanton* we play with our grief; *fond* foolishly affectionate
V, ii The palace of the Duke of York   4 *leave* leave off   5 *misgoverned*
unruly; *windows' tops* upper windows

115

 9   Which his aspiring rider seemed to know,
        With slow but stately pace kept on his course,
        Whilst all tongues cried, 'God save thee, Bolingbroke!'
        You would have thought the very windows spake,
        So many greedy looks of young and old
        Through casements darted their desiring eyes
        Upon his visage; and that all the walls
16   With painted imagery had said at once,
        'Jesu preserve thee! Welcome, Bolingbroke!'
        Whilst he, from the one side to the other turning,
        Bareheaded, lower than his proud steed's neck,
        Bespake them thus, 'I thank you, countrymen.'
        And thus still doing, thus he passed along.

DUCHESS
        Alack, poor Richard! Where rode he the whilst?

YORK
        As in a theatre the eyes of men,
24   After a well-graced actor leaves the stage,
25   Are idly bent on him that enters next,
        Thinking his prattle to be tedious,
        Even so, or with much more contempt, men's eyes
        Did scowl on gentle Richard. No man cried, 'God save
            him!'
        No joyful tongue gave him his welcome home,
        But dust was thrown upon his sacred head;
        Which with such gentle sorrow he shook off,
        His face still combating with tears and smiles,
33   The badges of his grief and patience,
        That, had not God for some strong purpose steeled
        The hearts of men, they must perforce have melted
36   And barbarism itself have pitied him.
        But heaven hath a hand in these events,

---

9 *Which . . . know* which seemed to know its ambitious rider 16 *With . . . imagery* painted with figures like a tapestry 24 *well-graced* graceful and well received 25 *idly* listlessly 33 *badges* tokens 36 *barbarism itself* even savages

To whose high will we bound our calm contents.   38
To Bolingbroke are we sworn subjects now,
Whose state and honor I for aye allow.   40
    [Enter Aumerle.]

DUCHESS
Here comes my son Aumerle.

YORK   Aumerle that was;
But that is lost for being Richard's friend,   42
And, madam, you must call him Rutland now.
I am in parliament pledge for his truth
And lasting fealty to the new-made king.   45

DUCHESS
Welcome, my son. Who are the violets now   46
That strew the green lap of the new-come spring?

AUMERLE
Madam, I know not, nor I greatly care not.
God knows I had as lief be none as one.

YORK
Well, bear you well in this new spring of time,
Lest you be cropped before you come to prime.
What news from Oxford? Do these justs and triumphs   52
    hold?

AUMERLE
For aught I know, my lord, they do.

YORK
You will be there, I know.

AUMERLE
If God prevent not, I purpose so.

YORK
What seal is that that hangs without thy bosom?
Yea, look'st thou pale? Let me see the writing.

AUMERLE
My lord, 'tis nothing.

---

38 *To . . . contents* we limit our wishes to calm content with heaven's high
will **40** *state* high rank **42** *that* that title **45** *fealty* loyalty **46–47** *Who
. . . spring* who are the new king's favorites **52** *Do . . . hold* will these
tourneys and victory celebrations be held

YORK   No matter then who see it.
I will be satisfied ; let me see the writing.

AUMERLE
I do beseech your grace to pardon me.
It is a matter of small consequence
Which for some reasons I would not have seen.

YORK
Which for some reasons, sir, I mean to see.
I fear, I fear –

DUCHESS   What should you fear ?

65   'Tis nothing but some bond that he is ent'red into
66   For gay apparel 'gainst the triumph day.

YORK
Bound to himself ? What doth he with a bond
That he is bound to ? Wife, thou art a fool.
Boy, let me see the writing.

AUMERLE
I do beseech you pardon me. I may not show it.

YORK
I will be satisfied. Let me see it, I say.
            He plucks it out of his bosom and reads it.
Treason, foul treason ! Villain ! traitor ! slave !

DUCHESS
What is the matter, my lord ?

YORK
Ho ! who is within there ?
            [Enter a Servant.]   Saddle my horse.
75   God for his mercy, what treachery is here !

DUCHESS
Why, what is it, my lord ?

YORK
Give me my boots, I say. Saddle my horse.
                              [Exit Servant.]
Now, by mine honor, by my life, by my troth,

---

65 *is ent'red into* has signed   **66** *'gainst* in anticipation of   **75** *God . . . mercy*
I pray God for his mercy

I will appeach the villain.   79
DUCHESS   What is the matter?
YORK
Peace, foolish woman.
DUCHESS
I will not peace. What is the matter, Aumerle?
AUMERLE
Good mother, be content. It is no more
Than my poor life must answer.
DUCHESS   Thy life answer?
YORK
Bring me my boots! I will unto the king.
        His Man enters with his boots.
DUCHESS
Strike him, Aumerle. Poor boy, thou art amazed. —   85
        [To York's Man]
Hence, villain! Never more come in my sight.
YORK
Give me my boots, I say!   *[Servant does so and exit.]*
DUCHESS
Why, York, what wilt thou do?
Wilt thou not hide the trespass of thine own?
Have we more sons? or are we like to have?
Is not my teeming date drunk up with time?   91
And wilt thou pluck my fair son from mine age
And rob me of a happy mother's name?
Is he not like thee? Is he not thine own?
YORK
Thou fond mad woman,
Wilt thou conceal this dark conspiracy?
A dozen of them here have ta'en the sacrament,
And interchangeably set down their hands,   98
To kill the king at Oxford.
DUCHESS   He shall be none;

---

79 *appeach* accuse publicly   **85** *him* i.e. the servant   **91** *teeming date* period
of childbearing   **98** *interchangeably . . . hands* signed reciprocally, so that
each had an indenture signed by all

100   We'll keep him here. Then what is that to him?
          YORK
                 Away, fond woman! Were he twenty times
                 My son, I would appeach him.
          DUCHESS   Hadst thou groaned for him
103   As I have done, thou wouldst be more pitiful.
                 But now I know thy mind. Thou dost suspect
                 That I have been disloyal to thy bed
                 And that he is a bastard, not thy son.
                 Sweet York, sweet husband, be not of that mind!
                 He is as like thee as a man may be,
                 Not like to me, or any of my kin,
                 And yet I love him.
          YORK   Make way, unruly woman!   *Exit.*
          DUCHESS
111   After, Aumerle! Mount thee upon his horse,
112   Spur post and get before him to the king,
                 And beg thy pardon ere he do accuse thee.
                 I'll not be long behind. Though I be old,
                 I doubt not but to ride as fast as York;
                 And never will I rise up from the ground
                 Till Bolingbroke have pardoned thee. Away, be gone!
                                                      [Exeunt.]

                              *

V, iii   *Enter the King [Henry IV] with his Nobles [Percy*
                  and others].
          KING HENRY
1   Can no man tell me of my unthrifty son?
                 'Tis full three months since I did see him last.
3   If any plague hang over us, 'tis he.
                 I would to God, my lords, he might be found.
                 Inquire at London, 'mongst the taverns there,

          100 *that* what they do   **103** *pitiful* full of pity   **111** *his horse* one of his
          horses   **112** *Spur post* ride fast
          V, iii Windsor Castle   **1** *unthrifty* prodigal   **3** *plague* calamity (as proph-
          esied by Carlisle)

For there, they say, he daily doth frequent,
With unrestrainèd loose companions,   7
Even such, they say, as stand in narrow lanes
And beat our watch and rob our passengers,   9
Which he, young wanton and effeminate boy,   10
Takes on the point of honor to support   11
So dissolute a crew.

PERCY
My lord, some two days since I saw the prince
And told him of those triumphs held at Oxford.

KING HENRY
And what said the gallant?

PERCY
His answer was, he would unto the stews,   16
And from the common'st creature pluck a glove
And wear it as a favor, and with that
He would unhorse the lustiest challenger.

KING HENRY
As dissolute as desperate! Yet through both
I see some sparks of better hope, which elder years
May happily bring forth. But who comes here?
        Enter Aumerle, amazed.

AUMERLE
Where is the king?

KING HENRY
What means our cousin, that he stares and looks
So wildly?

AUMERLE
God save your grace! I do beseech your majesty
To have some conference with your grace alone.

KING HENRY
Withdraw yourselves and leave us here alone.
                        [Exeunt Percy and Lords.]

---

7 *loose* wild   **9** *watch* night patrolmen; *passengers* wayfarers   **10** *Which* as to which; *wanton* 'sport'; *effeminate* self-indulgent   **11** *Takes on the* takes it as a   **16** *stews* brothels

What is the matter with our cousin now?

AUMERLE
For ever may my knees grow to the earth,
    [Kneels.]
My tongue cleave to my roof within my mouth,
Unless a pardon ere I rise or speak.

KING HENRY
Intended, or committed, was this fault?
34 If on the first, how heinous e'er it be,
To win thy after-love I pardon thee.

AUMERLE
Then give me leave that I may turn the key,
That no man enter till my tale be done.

KING HENRY
Have thy desire.
    [Aumerle locks the door.] The Duke of York knocks
    at the door and crieth.

YORK *[within]*
My liege, beware! look to thyself!
Thou hast a traitor in thy presence there.

KING HENRY
Villain, I'll make thee safe.
    [Draws.]

AUMERLE
Stay thy revengeful hand; thou hast no cause to fear.

YORK *[within]*
43 Open the door, secure foolhardy king!
44 Shall I for love speak treason to thy face?
Open the door, or I will break it open!
    [Enter York.]

KING HENRY
What is the matter, uncle? Speak.
Recover breath; tell us how near is danger,
That we may arm us to encounter it.

---

34 *on the first* in the first category, intended   43 *secure* overconfident 44
speak treason call you a fool

YORK

    Peruse this writing here, and thou shalt know

    The treason that my haste forbids me show.   50

AUMERLE

    Remember, as thou read'st, thy promise passed.

    I do repent me. Read not my name there.

    My heart is not confederate with my hand.

YORK

    It was, villain, ere thy hand did set it down.

    I tore it from the traitor's bosom, king.

    Fear, and not love, begets his penitence.

    Forget to pity him, lest thy pity prove   57

    A serpent that will sting thee to the heart.

KING HENRY

    O heinous, strong, and bold conspiracy!   59

    O loyal father of a treacherous son!

    Thou sheer, immaculate, and silver fountain,   61

    From whence this stream through muddy passages

    Hath held his current and defiled himself!

    Thy overflow of good converts to bad,   64

    And thy abundant goodness shall excuse

    This deadly blot in thy digressing son.   66

YORK

    So shall my virtue be his vice's bawd,

    And he shall spend mine honor with his shame,

    As thriftless sons their scraping fathers' gold.

    Mine honor lives when his dishonor dies,

    Or my shamed life in his dishonor lies.

    Thou kill'st me in his life; giving him breath,

    The traitor lives, the true man's put to death.

DUCHESS [within]

    What ho, my liege! For God's sake let me in!

KING HENRY

    What shrill-voiced suppliant makes this eager cry?

---

50 *haste* breathlessness from hurrying   **57** *Forget* forget your promise   **59** *strong* flagrant   **61** *sheer* pure   **64** *converts* changes   **66** *digressing* transgressing

DUCHESS *[within]*
> A woman, and thy aunt, great king. 'Tis I.
> Speak with me, pity me, open the door!
> A beggar begs that never begged before.

KING HENRY
> Our scene is alt'red from a serious thing,
80   And now changed to 'The Beggar and the King.'
> My dangerous cousin, let your mother in.
> I know she is come to pray for your foul sin.

YORK
> If thou do pardon, whosoever pray,
> More sins for this forgiveness prosper may.
> This fest'red joint cut off, the rest rest sound;
> This let alone will all the rest confound.
>   *[Enter Duchess.]*

DUCHESS
> O king, believe not this hardhearted man!
88   Love loving not itself, none other can.

YORK
89   Thou frantic woman, what dost thou make here?
> Shall thy old dugs once more a traitor rear?

DUCHESS
> Sweet York, be patient. Hear me, gentle liege.
>   *[Kneels.]*

KING HENRY
> Rise up, good aunt.

DUCHESS   Not yet, I thee beseech.
> For ever will I walk upon my knees,
> And never see day that the happy sees,
> Till thou give joy, until thou bid me joy
> By pardoning Rutland, my transgressing boy.

AUMERLE
> Unto my mother's prayers I bend my knee.
>   *[Kneels.]*

---

80 '*The . . . King*' acting out the ballad of King Cophetua and the beggar-maid   88 *Love . . . can* if he does not love his own son, he cannot love anyone else   89 *make* do

124

YORK

Against them both my true joints bended be.
  [Kneels.]
Ill mayst thou thrive if thou grant any grace !

DUCHESS

Pleads he in earnest ? Look upon his face.
His eyes do drop no tears, his prayers are in jest ;
His words come from his mouth, ours from our breast.
He prays but faintly and would be denied ;
We pray with heart and soul and all beside.
His weary joints would gladly rise, I know ;
Our knees still kneel till to the ground they grow.   106
His prayers are full of false hypocrisy ;
Ours of true zeal and deep integrity.
Our prayers do outpray his ; then let them have
That mercy which true prayer ought to have.

KING HENRY

Good aunt, stand up.

DUCHESS   Nay, do not say 'stand up.'
Say 'pardon' first, and afterwards 'stand up.'
An if I were thy nurse, thy tongue to teach,
'Pardon' should be the first word of thy speech.
I never longed to hear a word till now.
Say 'pardon' king ; let pity teach thee how.
The word is short, but not so short as sweet ;
No word like 'pardon' for kings' mouths so meet.

YORK

Speak it in French, king. Say 'Pardonne moi.'   119

DUCHESS

Dost thou teach pardon pardon to destroy ?
Ah, my sour husband, my hardhearted lord,
That sets the word itself against the word !
Speak 'pardon' as 'tis current in our land ;   123

---

106 *still kneel* (will) kneel continually   **119** *'Pardonne moi'* 'excuse me' – a
polite 'no'   **123** *as . . . land* as customarily used in English

124   The chopping French we do not understand.
        Thine eye begins to speak, set thy tongue there;
        Or in thy piteous heart plant thou thine ear,
127   That hearing how our plaints and prayers do pierce,
128   Pity may move thee 'pardon' to rehearse.

KING HENRY
    Good aunt, stand up.

DUCHESS   I do not sue to stand.
    Pardon is all the suit I have in hand.

KING HENRY
    I pardon him as God shall pardon me.

DUCHESS
    O happy vantage of a kneeling knee!
    Yet am I sick for fear. Speak it again.
    Twice saying 'pardon' doth not pardon twain,
    But makes one pardon strong.

KING HENRY   With all my heart
    I pardon him.

DUCHESS   A god on earth thou art.
        [Rises.]

KING HENRY
137   But for our trusty brother-in-law and the abbot,
138   With all the rest of that consorted crew,
        Destruction straight shall dog them at the heels.
        Good uncle, help to order several powers,
        To Oxford, or where'er these traitors are.
        They shall not live within this world, I swear,
        But I will have them, if I once know where.
        Uncle, farewell; and, cousin, adieu.
        Your mother well hath prayed, and prove you true.

DUCHESS
    Come, my old son. I pray God make thee new.
                    Exeunt [as Exton and Servant enter].

124 *The chopping French* the French phrase, in which the words change
their meaning   127 *pierce* (then pronounced to rhyme with *rehearse*)   128
rehearse repeat   137 *brother-in-law* the Duke of Exeter; *the abbot* of
Westminster   138 *consorted crew* conniving gang

Manet Sir Pierce Exton, & c. [Servant]. V, iv

EXTON
Didst thou not mark the king, what words he spake?
'Have I no friend will rid me of this living fear?'
Was it not so?

MAN   These were his very words.

EXTON
'Have I no friend?' quoth he. He spake it twice
And urged it twice together, did he not?   5

MAN
He did.

EXTON
And speaking it, he wishtly looked on me,   7
As who should say, 'I would thou wert the man
That would divorce this terror from my heart!'
Meaning the king at Pomfret. Come, let's go.
I am the king's friend, and will rid his foe.   *[Exeunt.]* 11

*

Enter Richard, alone.   V, v

RICHARD
I have been studying how I may compare
This prison where I live unto the world;
And, for because the world is populous,
And here is not a creature but myself,
I cannot do it. Yet I'll hammer it out.
My brain I'll prove the female to my soul,
My soul the father; and these two beget
A generation of still-breeding thoughts;   8
And these same thoughts people this little world,
In humors like the people of this world,   10

V, iv 5 *urged . . . together* emphasized it by repeating it   7 *wishtly* intently
11 *rid* get rid of
V, v The keep in Pomfret Castle 8 *still-breeding* constantly breeding
10 *In . . . world* the creatures of fancy have their peculiar dispositions as
real people do

For no thought is contented. The better sort,
As thoughts of things divine, are intermixed
13   With scruples, and do set the word itself
Against the word:
As thus, 'Come, little ones,' and then again,
'It is as hard to come as for a camel
17   To thread the postern of a small needle's eye.'
Thoughts tending to ambition, they do plot
Unlikely wonders – how these vain weak nails
May tear a passage through the flinty ribs
21   Of this hard world, my ragged prison walls;
22   And, for they cannot, die in their own pride.
Thoughts tending to content flatter themselves
That they are not the first of fortune's slaves,
25   Nor shall not be the last; like seely beggars
26   Who, sitting in the stocks, refuge their shame.
That many have, and others must sit there.
And in this thought they find a kind of ease,
Bearing their own misfortunes on the back
Of such as have before endured the like.
Thus play I in one person many people,
And none contented. Sometimes am I king:
Then treasons make me wish myself a beggar,
And so I am. Then crushing penury
Persuades me I was better when a king;
Then am I kinged again; and by and by
Think that I am unkinged by Bolingbroke,
And straight am nothing. But whate'er I be,
Nor I, nor any man that but man is,
With nothing shall be pleased till he be eased
41   With being nothing. *(The music plays.)* Music do I hear?
Ha – ha – keep time! How sour sweet music is

---

13 *scruples* doubts   13–14 *set ... word* find one passage of Scripture which
contradicts another   17 *postern* narrow gate   21 *ragged* rugged   22 *pride*
prime   25 *seely* simple-minded   26–27 *refuge ... That* find refuge for
their shame in the thought that   41 *being nothing* death

128

When time is broke and no proportion kept!
So is it in the music of men's lives.
And here have I the daintiness of ear
To check time broke in a disordered string;   46
But, for the concord of my state and time,
Had not an ear to hear my true time broke.
I wasted time, and now doth time waste me;
For now hath time made me his numb'ring clock: 50
My thoughts are minutes; and with sighs they jar   51
Their watches on unto mine eyes, the outward watch,   52
Whereto my finger, like a dial's point,   53
Is pointing still, in cleansing them from tears.
Now, sir, the sound that tells what hour it is
Are clamorous groans, which strike upon my heart,
Which is the bell. So sighs and tears and groans
Show minutes, times, and hours. But my time   58
Runs posting on in Bolingbroke's proud joy,
While I stand fooling here, his Jack of the clock.   60
This music mads me. Let it sound no more;
For though it have holp madmen to their wits,   62
In me it seems it will make wise men mad.   63
Yet blessing on his heart that gives it me!
For 'tis a sign of love, and love to Richard
Is a strange brooch in this all-hating world.   66
          Enter a Groom of the stable.

GROOM
    Hail, royal prince!   67
RICHARD   Thanks, noble peer.

---

46 *check* rebuke; *disordered* playing ahead of or behind the beat   50
numb'ring clock clock showing hours and minutes (not an hourglass)   51
jar tick   52 *watches* periods; *outward watch* clock face, with a play on
Richard's eyes, sleepless, peering outward   53 *dial's point* clock hand
58 *times* quarters and halves   60 *Jack of the clock* mannikin which strikes
the hours   62 *holp* helped   63 *wise* sane   66 *strange brooch* rare jewel;
all-hating world world where I am universally hated   67–68 *royal . . . dear*
(a royal was a coin worth 10s., a noble 6s. 8d.; the difference was ten groats,
a groat being fourpence)

The cheapest of us is ten groats too dear.
What art thou? and how comest thou hither,
70   Where no man never comes but that sad dog
That brings me food to make misfortune live?

GROOM

I was a poor groom of thy stable, king,
When thou wert king; who, travelling towards York,
With much ado, at length, have gotten leave
To look upon my sometimes royal master's face.
76   O, how it erned my heart when I beheld,
In London streets, that coronation day,
When Bolingbroke rode on roan Barbary,
That horse that thou so often hast bestrid,
80   That horse that I so carefully have dressed!

RICHARD

Rode he on Barbary? Tell me, gentle friend,
How went he under him?

GROOM

So proudly as if he disdained the ground.

RICHARD

So proud that Bolingbroke was on his back!
85   That jade hath eat bread from my royal hand;
86   This hand hath made him proud with clapping him.
Would he not stumble? would he not fall down,
Since pride must have a fall, and break the neck
Of that proud man that did usurp his back?
Forgiveness, horse! Why do I rail on thee,
Since thou, created to be awed by man,
Wast born to bear? I was not made a horse;
And yet I bear a burden like an ass,
94   Spurred, galled, and tired by jauncing Bolingbroke.
Enter one [Keeper] to Richard with meat.

---

70 *no . . . never* (an emphatic double negative); *sad dog* dismal fellow **76** *erned my heart* caused my heart to mourn **80** *dressed* groomed **85** *eat* eaten **86** *with clapping* by petting **94** *jauncing* making the horse prance, riding showily

KEEPER

Fellow, give place. Here is no longer stay.

RICHARD

If thou love me, 'tis time thou wert away.

GROOM

What my tongue dares not, that my heart shall say.

Exit Groom.

KEEPER

My lord, will't please you to fall to?

RICHARD

Taste of it first, as thou art wont to do.   99

KEEPER

My lord, I dare not. Sir Pierce of Exton,
Who lately came from the king, commands the contrary.

RICHARD

The devil take Henry of Lancaster, and thee!
Patience is stale, and I am weary of it.
       [Beats the Keeper.]

KEEPER

Help, help, help!
       The Murderers [Exton and Servants] rush in.

RICHARD

How now! What means Death in this rude assault?
Villain, thy own hand yields thy death's instrument.
       [Snatches a weapon from a Servant and kills him.]
Go thou and fill another room in hell.   107
       [Kills another.] Here Exton strikes him down.
That hand shall burn in never-quenching fire
That staggers thus my person. Exton, thy fierce hand
Hath with the king's blood stained the king's own land.
Mount, mount, my soul! thy seat is up on high;
Whilst my gross flesh sinks downward, here to die.
       [Dies.]

---

99 *Taste . . . first* (a taster to insure that food was not poisoned was a royal prerogative)   **107** *room* place

131

EXTON
As full of valor as of royal blood!
Both have I spilled. O, would the deed were good!
For now the devil, that told me I did well,
Says that this deed is chronicled in hell.
This dead king to the living king I'll bear.
Take hence the rest, and give them burial here.

[Exeunt.]

*

V, vi   [Flourish.] Enter Bolingbroke [as King], with the
             Duke of York [, other Lords, and Attendants].

KING
Kind uncle York, the latest news we hear
Is that the rebels have consumed with fire
3   Our town of Ciceter in Gloucestershire;
But whether they be ta'en or slain we hear not.
             Enter Northumberland.
Welcome, my lord. What is the news?

NORTHUMBERLAND
First, to thy sacred state wish I all happiness.
The next news is, I have to London sent
The heads of Oxford, Salisbury, Blunt, and Kent.
9   The manner of their taking may appear
At large discoursèd in this paper here.

KING
We thank thee, gentle Percy, for thy pains
And to thy worth will add right worthy gains.
             Enter Lord Fitzwater.

FITZWATER
My lord, I have from Oxford sent to London
The heads of Brocas and Sir Bennet Seely,
Two of the dangerous consorted traitors
That sought at Oxford thy dire overthrow.

V, vi Windsor Castle   3 *Ciceter* i.e. Cirencester   9 *taking* capture

KING

    Thy pains, Fitzwater, shall not be forgot.

    Right noble is thy merit, well I wot.

        Enter Henry Percy [and the Bishop of Carlisle].

PERCY

    The grand conspirator, Abbot of Westminster,

    With clog of conscience and sour melancholy   20

    Hath yielded up his body to the grave;

    But here is Carlisle living, to abide   22

    Thy kingly doom and sentence of his pride.

KING

    Carlisle, this is your doom:

    Choose out some secret place, some reverend room,   25

    More than thou hast, and with it joy thy life.   26

    So, as thou liv'st in peace, die free from strife;

    For though mine enemy thou hast ever been,

    High sparks of honor in thee have I seen.

        Enter Exton, with [Attendants bearing] the coffin.

EXTON

    Great king, within this coffin I present

    Thy buried fear. Herein all breathless lies

    The mightiest of thy greatest enemies,

    Richard of Bordeaux, by me hither brought.

KING

    Exton, I thank thee not; for thou hast wrought

    A deed of slander, with thy fatal hand,   35

    Upon my head and all this famous land.

EXTON

    From your own mouth, my lord, did I this deed.

KING

    They love not poison that do poison need,

    Nor do I thee. Though I did wish him dead,

    I hate the murderer, love him murderèd.

---

20 *With clog* under the crippling weight   **22** *abide* await   **25** *reverend room* place of religious retirement   **26** *joy* gladden   **35** *deed of slander* deed to rouse slanderous talk against the crown

The guilt of conscience take thou for thy labor,
But neither my good word nor princely favor.
43   With Cain go wander thorough shades of night,
And never show thy head by day nor light.
Lords, I protest my soul is full of woe
That blood should sprinkle me to make me grow.
Come, mourn with me for what I do lament,
48   And put on sullen black incontinent.
I'll make a voyage to the Holy Land
To wash this blood off from my guilty hand.
51   March sadly after. Grace my mournings here
In weeping after this untimely bier.   *[Exeunt.]*

---

43 *thorough* through   48 *incontinent* immediately   51 *Grace* dignify with
your presence

A selection of books published by Penguin is listed on the following pages.

For a complete list of books available from Penguin in the United States, write to Dept. DG, Penguin Books, 299 Murray Hill Parkway, East Rutherford, New Jersey 07073.

For a complete list of books available from Penguin in Canada, write to Penguin Books Canada Limited, 2801 John Street, Markham, Ontario L3R 1B4.

The Complete Pelican
SHAKESPEARE

To fill the need for a convenient and authoritative one-volume edition, the thirty-eight books in the Pelican series have been brought together.

THE COMPLETE PELICAN SHAKESPEARE includes all the material contained in the separate volumes, together with a 50,000-word General Introduction and full bibliographies. It contains the first nineteen pages of the First Folio in reduced facsimile, five new drawings, and illustrated endpapers. 9¾ × 7³⁄₁₆ inches, 1520 pages.

INTRODUCING
SHAKESPEARE
Third Edition

G. B. Harrison

Now a classic, this volume has been the best popular introduction to Shakespeare for over thirty years. Dr. G. B. Harrison discusses first Shakespeare's legend and then his tantalizingly ill-recorded life. Harrison describes the Elizabethan playhouse (with the help of a set of graphic reconstructions) and examines the effect of its complicated structure on the plays themselves. It is in the chapter on the Lord Chamberlain's Players that Shakespeare and his associates are most clearly seen against their background of theatrical rivalry, literary piracy, the closing of the playhouses because of the plague, the famous performance of *Richard II* in support of the Earl of Essex, and the fire that finally destroyed the Globe Theater.

SHAKESPEARE

Anthony Burgess

Bare entries in parish registers, a document or two, and a few legends and contemporary references make up the known life of William Shakespeare. Anthony Burgess has clothed these attractively with an extensive knowledge of Elizabethan and Jacobean England for this elaborately illustrated biography. The characters of the men Shakespeare knew, the influence of his life on his plays, and the stirring events that must have been in the minds of author, actors, and audience are engagingly described here by a writer who sees "Will" not as an ethereal bard but as a sensitive, sensual, and shrewd man from the provinces who turned his art to fortune in the most exciting years of England's history. "It was a touch of near genius to choose Mr. Burgess to write the text for a richly illustrated life of Shakespeare, for his wonderfully well-stocked mind and essentially wayward spirit are just right for summoning up an apparition of the bard which is more convincing than most"—David Holloway, *London Daily Telegraph*. With 48 plates in color and nearly 100 black-and-white illustrations.

PENGUIN ENGLISH LIBRARY

The Penguin English Library Series reproduces, in convenient but authoritative editions, many of the greatest classics in English literature from Elizabethan times through the nineteenth century. Each volume is introduced by a critical essay, enhancing the understanding and enjoyment of the work for the student and general reader alike. A few selections from the list of more than one hundred titles follow:

BEN JONSON: THREE COMEDIES
Edited by Michael Jamieson
VOLPONE, THE ALCHEMIST, BARTHOLOMEW FAIR

JOHN WEBSTER: THREE PLAYS
Edited by D. C. Gunby
THE WHITE DEVIL, THE DUCHESS OF MALFI,
THE DEVIL'S LAW-CASE

THREE JACOBEAN TRAGEDIES
Edited by Gāmini Salgādo
THE REVENGER'S TRAGEDY, *Cyril Tourneur*
THE WHITE DEVIL, *John Webster*
THE CHANGELING, *Thomas Middleton and William Rowley*

FOUR JACOBEAN CITY COMEDIES
Edited by Gāmini Salgādo
THE DUTCH COURTESAN, *John Marston*
A MAD WORLD, MY MASTERS, *Thomas Middleton*
THE DEVIL IS AN ASS, *Ben Jonson*
A NEW WAY TO PAY OLD DEBTS, *Philip Massinger*

THREE RESTORATION COMEDIES
Edited by Gāmini Salgādo
THE MAN OF MODE, *George Etherege*
THE COUNTRY WIFE, *William Wycherley*
LOVE FOR LOVE, *William Congreve*

Also works by Jane Austen, Charlotte Brontë, Emily Brontë, John Bunyan, Samuel Butler, Wilkie Collins, Daniel Defoe, Charles Dickens, George Eliot, Henry Fielding, Elizabeth Gaskell, Thomas Malory, Herman Melville, Edgar Allan Poe, Tobias Smollett, Laurence Sterne, Jonathan Swift, William Makepeace Thackeray, Anthony Trollope, Mark Twain, and others

PLAYS BY BERNARD SHAW

ANDROCLES AND THE LION

THE APPLE CART

ARMS AND THE MAN

BACK TO METHUSELAH

CAESAR AND CLEOPATRA

CANDIDA

THE DEVIL'S DISCIPLE

THE DOCTOR'S DILEMMA

HEARTBREAK HOUSE

MAJOR BARBARA

MAN AND SUPERMAN

THE MILLIONAIRESS

PLAYS UNPLEASANT
(WIDOWERS' HOUSES, THE PHILANDERER,
MRS WARREN'S PROFESSION)

PYGMALION

SAINT JOAN

SELECTED ONE ACT PLAYS
(THE SHEWING-UP OF BLANCO POSNET,
HOW HE LIED TO HER HUSBAND, O'FLAHERTY V.C.,
THE INCA OF PERUSALEM, ANNAJANSKA, VILLAGE WOOING,
THE DARK LADY OF THE SONNETS, OVERRULED,
GREAT CATHERINE, AUGUSTUS DOES HIS BIT,
THE SIX OF CALAIS)